THE MONSTER
UNDER THE BED

OTHER BOOKS BY ANTHONY GIANGREGORIO

THE DEAD WATER SERIES

DEADWATER
DEADWATER: Expanded Edition
DEADRAIN
DEADCITY
DEADWAVE
DEAD HARVEST
DEAD UNION
DEAD VALLEY

ALSO BY THE AUTHOR

DEAD RECKONING: DAWNING OF THE DEAD
DEAD END: A ZOMBIE NOVEL
DEAD TALES: SHORT STORIES TO DIE FOR
DEAD MOURNING: A ZOMBIE HORROR STORY
ROAD KILL: A ZOMBIE TALE
DEADFREEZE
DEADFALL
DEADRAGE
SOUL-EATER
THE DARK
RISE OF THE DEAD
DARK PLACES
REVOLUTION OF THE DEAD

The Monster Under The Bed

Anthony Giangregorio

ACKNOWLEDGMENTS

A big thanks to Roger Shieding, my mom, and my wife for helping with the finishing of this book; and to my two sons, Joseph and Domenic.

AUTHOR'S NOTE

This book was self-edited, and though I tried my absolute best to correct all grammar mistakes; there may be a few here and there. Please accept my sincerest apology for any errors you may find.

This is the second edition of this book.

Visit my website at www.undeadpress.com

THE MONSTER UNDER THE BED

FOREWORD

When someone asks you what a monster is, like me, you probably think of something with bulging eyes and slime or maybe something with two heads and ten eyes. Or maybe you think of one of the more classical monsters like Frankenstein or Dracula, or better yet, a zombie fresh from the grave.

But what about the monsters who live beside us every day? What about the child rapists and pedophiles who usually end up taking up residence in our own backyards?

And let's not forget the family unit itself.

Though many a comedian will joke about the eccentric uncle who would always want you to sit on his lap at holiday functions and bounce you up and down until you thought you'd be sick, or would always be the first one to volunteer for a sleepover, almost everyone alive knows what he was really about.

Sure it's fun to joke, but is it because we see these monsters day after day and so become immune to them? Of course most people will agree they're bad, but no one runs away screaming down the street when the pervert for a step-father comes home after boozing at the local bar and jumps into bed with his step-daughter.

Instead, it stays hidden in the closet, like the ugly sweater your wife got you for Christmas last year.

It's almost like, in some small way, they have been accepted as a part of our lives and are tolerated in some miniscule way.

If you saw a zombie walking down the street trying to rip out terrified people's throats, no one would hesitate to put a bullet in its head, so then why do we tolerate the perverts, pedophiles and the low-lifes who prey on children for prostitution and as part of the drug trade?

Just because these people look like other human beings doesn't make them human. Compassion for your fellow man and empathy is what makes each and every one of us human and connected. Not wanting to inflict pain on others is what makes us human.

So the next time you watch a horror movie about the bad old monster from the bottom of the lake, take a good look out your living room window at the house across the street.

Those monsters just might be closer than you think.

Anthony Giangregorio
May 2007

Chapter One

RUPERT WAS A monster, but not just any old monster.

Rupert was different; he had a heart.

Rupert was one of the many monsters that lived under the beds of children all across the world.

While Rupert's brethren would come out of their dimensional portals every evening, prepared for a night of trying to grab children's legs as they climbed into bed every night, Rupert had secretly wished he could just play with the children.

Rupert would hide every night, just watching the child getting ready for bed and then climbing into the bed above him, he always just wanted to just climb out and say: "Hi, I'm Rupert, would you like to play with me?"

He dreamed of having a friend of his very own, someone who would play games with him. The other monsters didn't agree with Rupert, of course. They said he was a dork and a loser for even imagining such a silly thing.

But Rupert knew he wasn't.

He knew he was just as good as any of the other monsters. In fact, on one such occasion, while having a drink after work with another monster, he had asked his associate: "But why? Why do we have to scare the children? Why can't we just be friends with them?"

His associate had just laughed, not believing what he had heard.

"Why? Because it's just not done, that's why. For as long as any of us can remember, we scare children and cause problems in the human realm. That's what we do. That's what we exist for."

Rupert had tried to argue some more, but the other monster had just put his clawed hand in front of Rupert's face, telling him he didn't want to hear about it.

Rupert had left then, still not agreeing with his fellow monster. Just because the rules said they had to scare children and cause problems didn't mean a thing to him. If the rules stunk, then change them, after all, the creator did give them all free will.

Now, there were many different classes of monsters. Rupert was part of the "scare" class. He and others like him would hide out under children's beds and in closets, waiting for the right time to scare them, but there were other classes, as well. There were the monsters that lived in the sewers of all the major cities and the gremlins that would make your car squeak just so. There were goblins that lived in people's cellars and fairies that mostly hung out in the woods and parks of all the major metropolitan cities. And there were dozens more that inhabited the human world despite the fact that humans never saw them.

One day, the head monster had called Rupert to a meeting. Rupert had strolled from his home, wondering why he had been summoned and had been worrying the entire time until finally reaching the building for monster affairs. He had walked into the head monster's office, his eyes looking at all the awards on the wall. There were dozens of commendations for all the quality scares the head monster had accomplished over his many years of service.

As he walked into the room, Rupert's eyes stared at them all, impressed. The head monster was on the phone and Rupert's eyes continued to scan all the documents, some of them jumping out at him.

He read a few of the more pronounced awards as he waited to be acknowledged. To Cecil Monster for Meritorious service. Made subject wet his pants on the first night, the first one read. Rupert was impressed. To scare a child so well as to make him pee his pants on the first night under his bed was a feat only a few monsters had ever accomplished. Usually it would take weeks of constant grabbing at ankles before the child would get to that stage of fear.

He read another: To Cecil B. Monster for exceptional service. Caused child to call for mommy on first night.

That made the big, blue, bushy eyebrows on Rupert's head go up. To make a child want his mommy after only the first night under his bed was a true accomplishment as most children were afraid to call out to their mommy's, fearing they would only get yelled at and told to just go back to sleep.

Rupert knew he stood in front of greatness, and wondered what this creature would want him for. Finally, Cecil put the phone down and looked up at Rupert.

Cecil resembled a large lizard, including the light shade of scales that covered all but the stomach of his body. His long tale waved behind him like a dog's.

With a quick clearing of his throat, he smiled. Rupert was pretty sure the smile was supposed to be charming, but with his razor sharp teeth and lack of lips, it only succeeded to make Rupert feel more uncomfortable.

"Ah, Rupert, it's nice to see you, my boy. Here, have a seat," Cecil said, waving Rupert to a chair sitting across from his desk.

Rupert nodded and did as he was asked.

Cecil steepled his fingers in front of himself and leaned back in his chair.

"Rupert, my boy, I have a problem," Cecil breathed, the sound reminding Rupert of a fog horn. "You see, one of my best monsters has taken sick and I need someone to fill in for him. I was hoping that creature would be you."

Rupert sat perfectly quiet, not really knowing what to say.

Cecil continued.

"As you know, there's a flu going around, monsteritous, I believe. More than half my staff is in bed sick. You are one of the few monsters on staff that seem to be fighting off the disease, so I need you to pick up some of the slack the other monsters are leaving behind." Cecil leaned forward in his chair. "Can you do that, my boy?"

Rupert nodded his head, pleased to help. "Yes, sir, whatever you need."

Cecil sat straight up and clapped his hand, sending a breeze at Rupert's head. The head monster's hands were almost double the size of a standard human's and his clap sent a cool breeze throughout the office.

"Wonderful, my boy. I knew you were a team player." He scribbled an address on a piece of paper from his notepad and handed it to Rupert. "This is the address. Be there at seven o' clock tonight, that way you can get a chance to get acclimated to the area."

Rupert stood up, prepared to leave, when Cecil stopped him. "One more thing, my boy. This child has proved to be a tough nut to crack, so don't be ashamed to pull out the big guns, all right?"

Rupert just nodded and Cecil waved him out of the room.

Rupert walked down the hallway of Monster Central and out into the street of his world. It was a beautiful day. It was overcast to the point there was nothing but grey clouds and it looked like it was going to rain at any second.

An absolutely perfect day.

That is, if you were a monster, of course.

While he walked down the sidewalk, he nodded to the other monsters that were outside with him today. A tall monster with six arms waved as he passed him, all three of its right arms coming up in greeting. Rupert nodded and smiled, continuing on his way. He looked down at the paper in his hand, reading the address. "112 Mockingbird Lane, Woonsocket, West Virginia," he read, turning a corner and moving further into Monster City.

He was on his way to see the Professor. He knew if he was going to scare this child the way he was supposed to, he would need some help. He didn't want to disappoint the head monster. If he did well on this assignment, then maybe he would get a promotion.

He smiled at that, avoiding a small creature that was walking in the middle of the sidewalk like he owned it. The creature was only the size of a large earth cat and had three eyes and two tails. Instead of fur it had spikes, like a porcupine. It knew most other monsters would avoid it, afraid of getting poked by its spikes. Rupert was in that category and he quickly stepped into the gutter as the small Catopine walked by.

The Catopine grinned, watching Rupert shuffle out of the way, then it continued down the street, ignoring him.

Rupert stepped back on the sidewalk and continued on. He was glad to see the Catopine receding down the street. The small creatures were notorious for wanting to start trouble and Rupert wasn't very confrontational.

In fact, he wished every creature could just be friends. He felt the world would be a better place, anyway; for both monster and human.

With a sigh flowing out of his mouth, he headed off down the street. Whenever he had a problem, the Professor would always help him with it and hopefully this time would be no different.

*   *   *

Rupert entered the small white building at the end of the street. From the outside no other monsters would ever imagine all the fabulous things that would occur inside the small building.

Inside, the Professor worked tirelessly to perfect the instruments to help his fellow monsters be better scarers. Rupert walked into the building, always enjoying all the sights and smells.

Test tubes lined one table against the wall and Rupert slowed and stopped to see what was inside each one today. Almost every time Rupert had visited, he had found the test tubes to be occupied by different shapes and forms.

Today was no different.

Rupert slowed as he stopped at the first test tube. Inside it was what looked like a bunny rabbit from the human realm, with the exception that this bunny had wings.

In the second test tube was a snake, but it appeared to have feet, like the Professor had crossed a millipede with a snake. He was about to see what the other tubes contained when the Professor stepped into the room from the rear of the building. He was an older monster, his gray hair predominant on his temple. The gray mixed with his blue fur to give him a more distinguished look. He had large ears, two sizes too big for his head and small blue tuffs of fur grew inside the ear canals. A big set of coke-bottle glasses sat on his large nose and bits of hair protruded from his nostrils, as well.

The Professor smiled when he saw Rupert. He was holding a large clipboard and he set it down on the corner of a desk and walked over to him.

"Ah, Rupert, it's so good to see you, how's the family?" He asked, holding out his hand for a quick handshake.

Rupert reached out with his clawed hand and the two creatures shook.

"Fine, Professor; thanks for asking. Dad is in Italy, hiding under a seven year old girl's bed and Mom is in the Netherlands. They've been on the same assignment for a while now."

The Professor clapped his hands together. "That's wonderful. And what can I do for you today? I assume this is not a social visit?"

Rupert pulled out the piece of paper he had received from Cecil.

"I just got a new assignment. The head monster gave it to me himself, so I don't want to mess it up. Do you have anything that might help me be a better scarer?"

The Professor's brow creased in thought, his forehead looking like the Nevada desert. "Perhaps," he nodded. "In fact, I'm pretty certain I know just the thing. Follow me into the back, will you?"

Rupert did as he was told, and in a few seconds the two monsters were standing in the middle of a giant machine shop. On every shelf sat different parts of machinery, most in dozens of pieces. The Professor was an absent-minded fellow and would start one project only to place it on one of the voluminous shelves and then start another one the next day.

The Professor walked to the farthest wall and reached up to the top shelf. He pulled down something long. Shambling over in his lackadaisical gait, he handed the tool to Rupert.

"What's this?" Rupert asked.

"It's an arm extension. See the hands on the end? You can use them to grab the child's legs before he makes it into the bed, thereby nullifying the standard jump."

Rupert nodded, understanding. A lot of children would take a running jump to get into bed at night; thereby avoiding the monster's grasping hands. With this new tool, he would be able to overcome that annoying obstacle.

"Thanks, Professor, this should work great." He reached into his pocket for some money. "How much do I owe you?"

The Professor thought it over for a moment, trying to decide what the tool was worth and then he just shrugged.

"Oh, I don't know; let's say three or four rodents?"

Rupert nodded in agreement. "Okay, that sounds fine." He reached into his fur to the small pocket on his stomach and pulled out four small creatures. While they looked like rats from the human world, similarity ended there. These small creatures had eight legs and had different color fur. They were the main food source for most of the creatures that lived on Rupert's world and so the small creatures were used as currency.

No one seemed to mind that they were intelligent.

As Rupert pulled out the first one, it blinked at the bright light of the room.

In a small squeaky voice it turned its head to look at Rupert.

"It's about time, I was wondering if you were ever going to take me out of there." The rat looked at the Professor and gestured to Rupert. "This guy is the biggest cheapskate on the planet. I was beginning to wonder if he was ever going to use me, in fact, I was ready to build a house in his pocket and start a family."

Rupert frowned at this. He hated when his money insulted him.

"Now you just hold on there, I'm not cheap, I'm frugal."

The rat's mouth creased into a smile. "Frugal? Buddy, you are so cheap you could squeeze a nickel from a penny."

Rupert held the rat at eye level and decided a retort was unnecessary. Instead, he just handed the little creature over to the Professor.

"Here, Professor, take this with you?" Then he reached into his pocket and pulled out three more of the small creatures. Each voluble rodent one had a wisecrack of his own to say about Rupert before the Professor took them from him and shoved them into one of his own voluminous pockets.

"Thank you, my boy; that will do fine. Ignore the currency; they're just disgruntled because they're food."

"I heard that. Screw you, too, old man!" A little voice yelled from the Professor's pocket. The Professor slapped his pocket, silencing the heckler and walked Rupert out of the building.

"Now, you just follow the instructions and you'll be fine, but be careful, the mechanism has a rather limited power source. Use it sparingly."

Rupert stopped at the doorway and turned to look at the Professor.

"Why, what would happen if I didn't?" He asked, curious, knowing some of the crazy things the Professor's inventions had done in the past.

The Professor shrugged. "Oh, not too much, it'll either just blow up in your face or stop working. Well, bye for now, and good luck." Then he closed the door, leaving Rupert to stand in the doorway with his mouth hanging open.

After a minute or two had passed, he regained his composure and waddled out onto the sidewalk. He had a busy day still ahead of him.

He had to pack and get his affairs in order before he left on his next assignment.

Although he didn't relish having to scare a poor child, he knew this could be his chance to move up the corporate ladder. Of course, that was so long as he didn't screw it up.

Chapter Two

*T*IMMY CONRAD CURLED up in his bed, ready to go to sleep. He was an average boy with light blonde hair and blue eyes. He liked Star Wars, Dragon Ball Z and Legos. He played Yu-gi-oh with his friends and watched the Teenage Mutant Ninja Turtles on television every Saturday morning. He enjoyed riding his bike and played soccer on Sundays with the neighborhood kids.

If someone was to ask his friends what he was like, they would say he was a fun, outgoing kid who loved life. But what they didn't know was a secret that Timmy had to keep deep down inside him.

A secret that ate at him like a cancer.

A secret that no eight year old boy should ever have to live with.

Timmy dreaded going to bed every night with every fiber of his being.

While the average eight year old hated to go to sleep, Timmy had more serious reasons for not wanting the night to come.

Almost every night, after his mother was in a valium induced state of sleep; his step-father would come into his room and touch him. He would always smell like cheap beer and Old Spice, two odors that would probably make Timmy vomit for the rest of his life.

His step-father would crawl into his bed and then rough hands would reach down his stomach. Timmy would always stay perfectly still, knowing that if he just remained motionless, it would soon be over.

His step-father would then let out a grunt and then just as silently as he had arrived, he would leave, leaving a wet spot on his sheets. Timmy would then lay alone in the dark, crying. He missed his real father, who had died in a car accident when he was only five. A drunk driver had crossed the yellow line, taking his father, Robert Conrad, away from him forever. The drunk had survived, as they so often do, and was even now in jail, paying for his crime.

But his father would be dead forever.

The man would be free by Timmy's tenth birthday; back on the street to live his life.

Meanwhile, his real dad would still be dead.

About six months ago, his mother had met another man, named David. David worked in pharmaceuticals and had immediately taken a shine to Timmy. Less than a month ago he had married his mother and had moved into their house.

It had taken less than a week before he had first shown up in the darkest hours of the night in Timmy's room. Timmy didn't totally understand what he did at night under the covers, but he knew it made him feel dirty and unclean…and embarrassed.

David had told him to keep quiet, that no one would understand and that he could lose his mom like he had lost his dad if he talked. So he kept quiet, pushing the shame further down inside himself.

If that wasn't bad enough, when David got really drunk, he would take it out on Timmy, slapping him around until Timmy was able to escape his clutches and hide under his bed or in a closet.

His mom was always high on valiums or some other drug. She had first started taking the medicine after his dad had died, not knowing how to cope with the loss of her husband. She had fallen into a pit of despair and drugs which had only become worse once she met David. Her new husband was able to get her any drugs she wanted and he did just that, keeping her in a drug induced haze almost all the time.

He liked her like that, she was easier to control.

The few times she would come out of her delirium, Timmy would enjoy being with his mom, remembering how things had been before his father had died. But then she would take something new and the mom he knew would disappear again, lost to the drugs and pills.

Timmy would hide in his closet sometimes, too afraid to get out. It was warm and safe in there, away from the troubles no eight year old should have to face.

His friend Bobby told him he should be scared of the closet, that there were monsters living in there, as well as under his bed.

Timmy would ignore him.

Compared to the monster he had to face every night, a real monster would be a nice change of pace.

Sometimes Timmy would daydream that a monster would arrive in his room one night and take his step-dad away, so he could never touch him again.

But he knew that could never happen. Monsters weren't real; at least the make- believe ones weren't.

With a tremble to his lip and a quicker beating of his young heart, Timmy crawled into bed. He prayed this would be one of the nights his step-father would stay passed out on the couch, not visiting him in the wee hours of the night.

His leg dangled over the bed, hanging out from the blanket. He was unafraid of the dreaded monster under the bed grabbing his leg and pulling him down with it. In fact, he almost welcomed it.

Anything was better than the Hell he had to live with every night when he turned off the light. Reaching over to his nightstand, he picked up a new copy of Daredevil. His mother had brought the comic book home the day before and Timmy had already read it twice from cover to cover. He opened it now, prepared to try to stay up for as long as possible. As long as his light stayed on, his step-father would leave him alone. He started to read the comic, becoming lost in the world of superheroes, where evil doers received their just desserts and the small boy lived happily ever after.

When he had finished the comic, his eyes were droopy and he knew he couldn't stay awake anymore. He decided it was time to turn off the light and go to bed.

Doing just that, he pulled the chain on the lamp next to his bed, casting the room in shadows. He sent a prayer to his father in Heaven, wondering if he was watching him and thinking if he was up there somewhere, then why was he letting bad things happen to him?

Then he closed his eyes, his breathing slowing, his pulse pounding in his ears from fright.

In time he drifted off to a restless sleep, dreams of his father and him playing in the park, happy, while his mother laid out a picnic lunch on a blanket for the three of them. Dogs played Frisbee with their owners and other children ran around them, playing tag with each other.

He laughed and played while high above him, a bright sun filled with hope shone down on them all.

CHAPTER THREE

*R*UPERT HAPPILY MADE his way down the sidewalk; his destination was his apartment building. The building was modeled a lot like an apartment complex from the human realm, except where human buildings were built straight up into the sky, his building went down into the earth.

Only the top floor was above ground, the other ten floors dug deep into the earth. It was just the nature of monsters. They enjoyed everything dank and dark.

But not Rupert though, he liked the sun on his face and the feeling of the wind as it ruffled his purple fur. He knew enough to keep such things to himself, though, and so not risk making himself more of an oddball then he already was.

He entered his building and walked through the lobby. There was a desk near the elevator and the concierge sat quietly reading a magazine.

"Hey, Ralph, how's things?" Rupert asked politely.

The creature that could be best described as a giant snail turned its head toward Rupert. With a voice that sounded like he was speaking underwater, Ralph shrugged (which was a feat in itself, considering he had no shoulders) and said:

"Hello there, Rupert. You want to know how I'm doing? Please, don't get me started. The misses says she wants to go on a vacation. Says I don't take her anywhere. And my oldest needs braces. And this shell is getting too small for me. How can I afford a new shell on a doorman's salary, I ask you?"

Rupert had pressed the elevator call button and was thankful when the door chimed open. With a wave he quickly stepped inside the car.

"Gee, Ralph, I'm really sorry about all that, good luck with everything." Then the elevator doors mercifully closed, cutting off Ralph's retort.

The doors of the elevator were a polished stainless steel type metal. Rupert couldn't help but check himself out. To an earth child he would look similar to a teddy bear, with the exception he was a light purple with very sharp claws and fangs and one droopy eye. Despite his appearance, though, he really was a big teddy bear, only wanting to be friends with everyone.

As the car shot downward, Rupert mentally decided to take the backdoor out of the building, not wanting to run into Ralph again. He just needed to pack a few things before he left on his new assignment. He needed the usual items, toothbrush, a brush for his fur, and some reading material to while away the time until the child would go to bed.

Just because he was a monster didn't mean he couldn't have good hygiene.

The elevator stopped at his floor and he stepped out into the gloomy hallway. No windows could be seen, and for light there just one flickering fluorescent bulb on the ceiling.

He started walking down the quiet hallway, slowing before he reached his door. He wanted to be as quiet as possible, not alerting his neighbor to his presence.

With his hand on his doorknob to enter his apartment, the door across the hall opened and he cringed.

His heart was already sinking in his chest as he turned around, his head low, to see the creature standing in the doorframe. She was wearing silky lingerie that became see-thru as Rupert looked at her silhouetted by the light coming from the inside of her apartment.

She was older than Rupert, the age difference similar to a grandmother to a teenager. She had been trying to get Rupert to come over for coffee ever since he had arrived in the building. Rupert repressed a shiver and looked up at her, smiling.

She was a sweet old monster and just needed to go after men her own age or at least born in the same century.

"Hello, Mrs. Mellanger, how are you today?" Rupert asked nicely.

Mrs. Mellanger resembled a grizzly bear with white fur and big lips that were now painted a dark red. Her fur hung down around her body, reminding Rupert of clothes that were to big for her and her makeup made her look like a cheap harlot.

She batted her eyes at Rupert and smiled, showing the fangs underneath those painted lips. "I'm lonely, Rupert, why don't you come over and visit with me?" She purred.

Rupert leaned against his door and folded his arms across his chest.

He sighed. "Look, Mrs. Mellanger, we've been over this. Your kind eats my kind; in fact, your kind eats anything if it's breathing. After you have your way with me, you'll just eat me and that will really put a damper on my future plans."

She pouted and moved into what she thought was a more sensual position. Rupert watched her and could taste his lunch in his mouth.

"But, my dear boy, think of the fun we'll have until then."

Rupert opened his door with his clawed hand behind his back and started to slip inside his apartment.

"Like I said before, thanks, but no thanks. Look, I gotta go. I've got a job to get to, see ya later." He closed the door then, her face disappearing from view. He caught her hurt visage as his door clicked shut, and despite the fact that she was a ravenous carnivore, he still felt just a little bad for her.

After all, in the end, all she really wanted was some company, a friend to tell her hopes and desires to.

And when she was done, of course, she'd eat them.

Rupert checked his phone messages and packed a bag. Ten minutes later he was ready to leave. He tossed the bag over his shoulder and cracked open the front door. Mrs. Mellanger's door was closed and he quickly stepped into the hallway, and with a soft click of his door, ran down the hallway as fast as he could.

Just before he made it to the stairwell, he heard her door open again, but by that time he was into the stairwell and on to the next floor, where he planned to catch the elevator.

Taking the stairs three at a time, he opened the fire door, stepped into the new hallway, and then moved to the elevator. After that it took only a moment to reach the lobby and then slip out of the elevator and creep to the side door and out the back, thereby avoiding Ralph, the creature never seeing him. As he walked down the street, heading for Portal Control, he wondered about all the people he knew. There was Ralph, the Professor and Mrs. Mellanger to name a few and as he thought of them, he couldn't help but wonder why people said he was the strange one.

Weaving through the streets of Monster City, Rupert walked the few blocks to Portal Control. The building came into view from his walk after only the first block had passed under his feet. Portal Control was the life's blood of Monster City. The tall building could be seen from almost anywhere in the massive metropolis.

This was where the miniature black hole was maintained.

The black hole allowed the monsters to travel from their dimension to Earth. The only way back was to be at the precise place at the precise time when the portal would reopen. If you missed it, then you were stuck on Earth forever, or at least until you could hook up with another monster and ride his portal back home.

Another convenient device only the more successful scarers had was a call button. Simply press the button to summon a Portal and then off you go, back to the home world.

Despite all these precautions, every now and then one of his fellow monsters would disappear from a job. No one ever knew what had happened to them. When a rescue party would be sent each time, all that could be found was a few extra dust-bunnies under the bed.

These monsters were the equivalent to being lost at sea and were mourned. None had ever returned.

Rupert tried not to think of these things, instead focusing on the positive. If he stuck to the monster's handbook and did what was required of him, then he would be home safely in a few weeks--maybe less if he scared the child quickly-- and ready for a new assignment.

Upon reaching the Portal building, he stepped inside. A security guard stood in front of a large desk that was in the middle of a low wall that went to both the left and right sides of the large room. Next to the desk was a gate. This was the only way to enter the actual Portal. First you had to go through security, similar to what humans did when they would fly on an airplane.

Rupert stepped into the line, waiting his turn. In front of him was an old monster that looked to be in her eighties. She resembled a giant caterpillar, with the exception of a white beehive hairdo and wire rimmed glasses that were on a chain if she needed to take them off. The security guard was checking her shoes, making sure there were no explosives inside. The creature behind her, a large slug, waited impatiently.

Finally the slug spoke up.

"Now come on, is that really necessary? She's eighty years old for the Creator's sake. I would bet my life she's not a terrorist. I'm going to miss my portal if you don't hurry up," the slug said unhappily.

The security guard stopped what he was doing and looked up at the slug. The guard best resembled an iguana, right down to the flicking tongue.

"Look, pal, I'm just doing my job. Ever since the earthworms from Dirac tried to blow up the portal we're on a heightened alert. Remember 12-25, man."

The slug looked taken aback. "12-25? What does the Earth Christmas have anything to do with me missing my portal?"

The guard finished with the caterpillar's shoes and handed it back to her. It had taken a while because she had sixteen feet and the guard felt he needed to check everyone.

The guard shrugged. "Nothing, actually, I just thought spouting some numbers would make me sound more important. Look, buddy, everyone knows you're supposed to show up for portal travel at least two hours early. I'm sorry if you're running late, but there's nothing I can do. Now we're not going to have a problem here, are we?" At his last word three more iguanas arrived from a side door. The slug saw these monsters and decided he wasn't in the mood for a cavity search today and backed down.

"No officer, I'm okay. Take as long as you want."

The guard grinned, his tongue slipping out to sense the air and then slipping back inside his mouth. Then he continued with the old lady caterpillar.

Rupert watched all this attentively; just glad he wasn't the one under the spotlight. Eventually, he made it through the gate. They had only taken half of his stuff this time, only leaving him his toothbrush. They had taken his toothpaste and brush saying they could be somehow used as weapons. He had just nodded. Who did they think he was, MacGyver?

He had watched the Earth show while on one of his assignments. The boy had watched it all the time and Rupert had peeked out from under the bed and watched himself. How you could make a jet pack out of a rubber elastic, a clothes-pin and a can of mayonnaise, he never knew, but it was still fun to watch.

He moved over to the portal line, waiting his turn. There was a large platform in the center of the room. The front wall was a giant view of space, the stars swirling around the black hole. Next to the platform a funny looking creature that resembled a giant mouse with glasses and a lab coat stood over a computer that was part machine and part organic. He would turn a few knobs and press a few buttons after the traveler would step on the platform, and after a flash of light, the traveler would be sent through the portal at an already predestined location.

All locations were either under beds or in closets, with fail safes in case the bed had been moved or the closet door was open. If they were being sent to a city, then the portal would usually open in an alley or a dumpster, somewhere private.

Finally it was Rupert's turn and he stepped onto the platform. The mouse barely noticed him; his job was to move the cattle back and forth, not to make nice with the clients. Rupert could feel a hum in his feet and his teeth started to hurt. Then he felt queasy and there was a bright flash of light in front of his eyes.

Then he knew nothing as he was sent through the portal to his new assignment.

In a matter of seconds, thousands of light-years and dimensions would be traversed, and if all went well, he would arrive in one piece under his new assignment's bed.

So with nothing to do for the next few seconds, Rupert just metaphorically laid back and enjoyed the ride.

19

Chapter Four

RUPERT OPENED HIS eyes, but he was still a little disoriented. As his vision cleared, he realized he was under a bed. Dust bunnies were everywhere; sticking to his purple fur and making him want to sneeze. The room was dark and he poked his head out from under the bed to try to see his surroundings better. From the first look around the room, he knew he was in the correct place. Posters of Spiderman and some other cartoons with yellow creatures and some with playing cards littered the walls from one end to the other. In the wan light of the room, he noticed a comic book lying on the floor of the bedroom. It had fallen off the nightstand to land upside down on the wooden floor.

He had already decided if the child was asleep then this night was a bust. The best time to get children was just before they got into bed and immediately afterward. That was when their little minds were going a mile a minute and they were most susceptible to being scared.

Rupert laid his head down on one of his furry arms, already bored. He reached for the comic book and opened it. His kind had excellent eyesight and was able to take in the slightest amount of light and amplify it. Most of the monsters in Monster City could. You had to be able to see in the dark if you were going to scare children after the lights went out.

He lay there quietly, flipping through the pages of the comic book. He couldn't read the writing because he had never bothered to learn the foreign Earth language, but he admired the pictures of a red man running around the city of New York fighting what looked to be other men in costumes. He liked New York. In fact, he had some extended family working there.

He looked up at the clock on the nightstand and saw it was a little past two in the morning. The boy above him was sleeping soundly, his soft breathing floating down to Rupert. Sometimes the portals were off on the arrival time. Still, only five hours off wasn't that bad when you were catapulted across dimensions of time and space.

Then the bedroom door creaked open and a silhouette of a man stood quietly in the door frame. Rupert watched the man sway back and forth for a few seconds and after a moment's hesitation, he stepped into the room.

The man's bare feet made almost no sound in the silence of the room and a second later the bed springs creaked as the man climbed into the boy's bed.

Rupert lay underneath, puzzled. This was odd behavior even for humans. He had seen the children run into their parent's bed screaming when he would scare them and the children would think they had just had a bad dream, but the parent never would enter the child's room and climb into bed with them.

He heard a rustling of bed clothes and then he heard odd sounds. The boy started to moan in his sleep, not happy about something. He kept telling the man, (who Rupert assumed was his father), to stop what he was doing. The man raised his voice harshly and the boy grew quiet. Only a few minutes had passed when the man stood up and left the room.

Once the door was closed, Rupert heard the boy crying. His sobbing was quiet, like the child was crying into his pillow, and Rupert wondered what was wrong. Out of all his years as a scarer, this had never happened before. He decided to break protocol and see what was happening with the child. He knew if he was found out by the head monster, he would be in for a serious reprimand, but his heart was just too big for him to ignore the child's cries.

Slowly, Rupert crawled out from under the bed, careful not to make any noise. One special ability all monsters had was that only children could see them. Adults were not able to perceive a monster even when it was standing right in front of them. That's why for hundreds of years, if not longer, parents never believed their children about monsters in their rooms.

It was physically impossible for them to see Rupert and his kind.

Rupert stood to his full six-foot five tall stature. Only a mix of what humans would call magic allowed him to fit under the bed with room to spare. If it wasn't for their use in the quantum field, monsters would never be able to hide in closets and under beds, it would be scientifically impossible.

In the darkened room the boy saw nothing, his face buried into his pillow.

Rupert hovered over him, not quite knowing what to do, and then decided to just pat the boy's shoulder.

Pat, pat, pat, pat.

The boy realized someone was in his room, perhaps thinking his mother had come in to comfort him. He stopped crying then, and with continuing sniffles, he reached over and turned on the lamp on his nightstand.

His face went slack and his mouth fell open as he stared into Rupert's big eyes.

Rupert didn't know quite what he should do, so he smiled. The only problem was Rupert was a monster, and when he smiled, he bared his fangs, his mouth curling up into a feral grin.

Any adult would have been scared at the sight of Rupert with his fangs bared and an eight year old boy was no match.

The boy screamed.

"Ahhhh, a monster! There's a monster in my room!" He yelled, sitting up in his bed, his eyes looking for an escape. But there was none. Rupert was directly in front of the door and the boy was helpless, so he dove under the blankets, making sure that all of his appendages were safe inside the covers.

Rupert frowned, knowing he could now not touch the boy.

This was one of the rules of being a monster under the bed that was sacrilege. No child can be harmed as long as he is fully under the bed covers.

Rupert stood there, unsure of what to do. His mouth opened, like he was going to say something, but then he closed it again.

Suddenly, the bedroom door was thrown open and the boy's father stood in the doorway.

"Timmy, for God's sake, it's almost three in the damn morning. Go to sleep."

Timmy shook his head under the covers, too afraid to look.

"No way, David, there's a monster in my room and he's gonna eat me. I just know it."

David stood there, not more than three feet from Rupert, but it was simply impossible for David to see him.

David shrugged; his hangover in full effect. "Jesus kid, I'm telling you there's nothing in here, now if you don't shut up, I'm going to get my belt. You got it?"

There was a muffled assent from the covers and David stepped out of the room and slammed the door shut. The room remained quiet for almost three minutes, Rupert not moving a muscle the entire time. The cat was out of the bag so to speak, so he might as well introduce himself. Maybe this could be the time he made a friend he could play with.

Timmy poked his eyes out of the sheets and screamed quietly again, quickly covering up his head again. Rupert decided enough was enough so he spoke up.

"Ummm. Hello there, I'm Rupert. I've been assigned as your monster. I'm supposed to be under your bed, but I heard you crying and I wanted to see if you were okay. I'm really sorry I scared you."

At first nothing happened, but slowly Timmy lowered the blanket from around his head. "You mean you're not here to eat me?"

Rupert laughed, a low throaty growl coming from his throat. "Oh my, no. In fact, the worst we monsters can do is grab your feet a little. But in the end we still have to let go. Those are the rules."

Timmy looked at Rupert, his eyes wide with amazement. "You mean you really are real? I'm not imagining you?"

"Well, I hope not," Rupert said. "I'm as real as you."

He sat down on the bed, nearly causing the side to break under his weight.

"Was that your father that was in here?" Rupert asked.

Timmy shook his head no. "Nah, that's David, he's my step-dad and he's a jerk…especially when I'm sleeping and he comes in to…see me." He hesitated the last part. "My real dad died when I was little. I miss him a lot."

Rupert nodded, understanding. "Yes, I know what you mean. My parents are far away from here, too, and I miss them everyday. Though I don't think it's quite the same." He held out his furry paw for Timmy to take. Timmy took one look at the talons at the end of the big paw-like hand and shrunk back.

"Don't be scared. I won't hurt you. I promise. Here, shake on it."

Timmy hesitated for a moment, but like most eight year olds, he was a trusting soul. He took Rupert at his word that he was friendly. He reached out and shook the massive paw, his small hand becoming lost in the fur. They pumped three times and then Rupert released Timmy's hand.

"There, now that we've shook on it, we have to be friends."

"Okay, that's fine with me," Timmy said.

Rupert looked at Timmy, his furry face creasing in what to him would be considered a frown.

"Timmy, can I ask you a question?"

Timmy nodded yes.

"What was your step-dad doing in here earlier?"

Timmy seemed to cringe at the question and seemed to become smaller as he shrank back into his pillows.

"I don't want to talk about it," he snapped.

Rupert nodded. "Okay, we don't have to talk about it now, but can we talk about it another time?"

Timmy thought for a second, small creases in his forehead appearing as he concentrated. Finally, he sat a little taller, and relaxed.

"Maybe, but just as long as we don't have to now."

"Deal," Rupert said. "Hey, you want to play a game?"

Timmy nodded happily. "Sure, okay."

The two new friends played games long into the night. When Rupert saw Timmy's eyes barely able to stay open, he put him back into his bed and covered him up. With dropping eyes, Timmy looked up at Rupert.

"Will I see you tomorrow night?" He asked sleepily.

Rupert nodded, his fur moving with the motion. "Yes, you will. I'll be here right after it gets dark."

"Okay, I'll see you then, night," the boy said.

Rupert patted Timmy's blanket and smiled. Then he crawled under the bed and waited for the portal to take him back home. He had done all he could for the night, more than he should have, actually.

A little while later, the portal began to form after all the safety checks had been initiated so the opening wouldn't be discovered

When it finally came, Rupert fell into its embrace, already looking forward to the next night when he would get to see Timmy again.

Outside Timmy's room, the floorboards creaked as David walked around the house. His hangover was killing him and when Timmy had screamed, he had thought the boy was going to ruin everything by opening his big mouth.

Taking another drink from his warm bottle of beer, his mind wrestled with ways to ensure the continued cooperation of his step-son.

With a malevolent grin on his lips, he went back to the kitchen to grab another bottle of beer.

One more, he thought, and then it would finally be time for bed.

CHAPTER FIVE

*T*HE NEXT NIGHT, Timmy was getting ready for bed. His mother was passed out in her bedroom, sprawled out on her bed. She had drunk wine with supper, and had then popped a couple of her valiums, the concoction putting her into a deep sleep that would last for the rest of the night.

Timmy paused by her bedroom and decided to walk inside her room. His mother's light-brown hair was covering her face and he gently brushed it away.

He missed her more than she would ever know. Although she might be in the house every day, she was still a million miles away. Timmy remembered all the fun they used to have together, playing games and sometimes just watching television together; both of them waiting for his dad to get home from work.

Now, when he looked down at his mother, he saw a hollow shell.

His head turned suddenly at the sound of a breaking bottle. Walking back into the hallway, he stopped at the end. From where he stood, he could see his living room clearly. His step-father was sprawled lazily out on the couch, a beer in his left hand. Next to him, on the coffee table, were five or six empty beer bottles. The sound Timmy had heard was the vase that had sat on the end-table next to the couch. His step-father had knocked it over with his free hand and now crystal shards covered the floor, reflecting the light from the television like a thousand stars.

Timmy backed away from where he was standing, taking extra care to be as quiet as possible. He was hoping Rupert would be under his bed when he got to his room. He hoped that Rupert could protect him from his step-dad.

He silently crept back to his room and ran inside, closing his door behind him. He ran over to the bed and then dropped down onto the floor.

A purple, furry face peeked out at him.

"Hi, Rupert, I'm glad you came back," Timmy said happily while backing away from the bed so Rupert could climb out. Timmy watched the monster slide out from under the bed like he had no bones. Once his form was entirely out, Rupert's body filled out to its actual size.

"Cool, how did you do that?" Timmy asked; his eyes wide with glee.

Rupert shrugged. It would take way to long to explain the dynamics of relative space and quantum mechanics to an eight-year-old, so he fell back on his old excuse.

"It was magic." Then he changed the subject. "So what do you want to do tonight?"

Timmy shrugged. "I don't know, do you like Playstation?"

Rupert scratched his head. "What's that?"

Timmy ran over to the other side of the room and turned on the small, twelve-inch, color television. Then he connected a few wires and turned on the video game system. When it was up and running, he showed Rupert how to play. At first it was complicated for the monster, his paws being far too large for the controller, but in time he got the hang of it and the two played game after game.

Timmy looked at the clock, seeing it was almost twelve midnight, hours after his supposed bedtime. He put down his controller and turned to Rupert.

"It's late, I need to get to bed" He said while rubbing his eyes. "If my step-dad finds out I'm still up he'll whip me good. Will you be back tomorrow night?"

Rupert looked down at the small boy sitting next to him on the bed. He looked so small and fragile and Rupert felt his heart opening to the boy.

He nodded. "You bet I will."

Sounds of footsteps outside the bedroom door caused Rupert to get up and quickly slide under the bed. Timmy ran to the television and turned it off. The room was thrown into darkness and Timmy jumped into his bed and pulled the covers over himself.

The door creaked open.

Timmy knew who it was and his blood ran cold. Rupert and he had talked while they had been playing video games, and although Timmy had been vague on what happened to him almost every night, Rupert had understood that something was bothering the boy deeply.

Rupert had given him some advice.

He had told the boy that sometimes no matter how scared you might be, you had to stand up for yourself or for others.

Timmy thought about those words now as his step-father stumbled into the room.

David walked over to Timmy's bed and stopped when the room was suddenly lit by the dull glow of the lamp on the nightstand, the shadows receding into the ether.

Timmy's hand was still on the switch.

"What the... Timmy, what are you doing? Turn that damn lamp off."

"No. Not tonight, David, no more. I don't want you coming into my room anymore." Inside, Timmy was so scared he thought he might pee himself, but he tried to stay strong, like Rupert had told him he should.

"In fact, when I go to school tomorrow, I'm going to tell my teacher what you do to me, or better yet, I'll go to Boston and tell my Grandpa. When he finds out, he'll beat you up and send you to jail. What you do to me is wrong and I won't let you do it anymore."

David's eyes went wide with both shock and anger.

He reached across the few feet that separated them and grabbed the boy by the arm. Timmy let out a small shriek from the pain, too surprised by the action to escape.

"Listen up you, little shit. If you say anything, I'll beat you to within an inch of your life. You hear me?"

Timmy swallowed hard, at the moment too afraid to answer. That was when a form materialized behind David.

Rupert had explained to Timmy how adults couldn't see him, but he was still there for moral support for the boy.

Timmy yanked his arm free and jumped off the bed. "No way, leave me alone, you big jerk!"

David's face creased into rage as he leaned over the bed while trying to recapture Timmy. "Damn it, come here, you little bastard! When I get my hands on you," he said, falling onto the bed, off balance.

Timmy ran around him and out of the room. He ran into the kitchen and opened the cabinet under the sink. With a little difficulty, he squeezed into the cupboard and closed the door behind him. For the first few seconds, nothing but his breathing and his heart beating filled his ears, but then the sound of heavy footsteps could be heard.

Cursing and sounds of furniture being moved around penetrated the cupboard doors. His step-dad was looking for him. At the moment, David was in the living room, looking through the closet at the far end of the house, but in time he would work his way to the kitchen. Timmy didn't want to think about what would happen then.

Minutes passed with the sounds of crashing continuing.

Then he heard his mother's voice coming from her bedroom.

"David, is everything all right? What's all that noise about? Is Timmy okay?" She asked; her voice groggy from sleep and drugs.

David stopped searching for Timmy, answering her with a: "Everything's fine, dear. I just lost my keys."

"Are you coming to bed? Do you need my help?" She asked, though the possibility that she would actually get up out of bed was slim. Still, it was enough to make David realize he needed to find Timmy quick and end his little revolt.

Cursing under his breath, David realized he better placate her, so he left the living room and went to his bedroom, where his wife was waiting.

Timmy heard muffled talking and decided if he was going to try and escape from David, it was now or never.

Not thinking it through, and too scared to face his step-dad, he ran into his room and closed the door, careful that it made no sound.

As quickly as he could, he got dressed, taking an extra moment to grab all his money from his Batman coin bank. Rupert appeared from under the bed, his face looking worried.

"Timmy, what are you doing? Where do you think you're going? It's past midnight." Rupert said quietly.

With tears rolling down his cheeks and his arms trembling from fright, Timmy started shoving clothes into a backpack.

"I'm running away, that's what I'm doing. If David finds me, he's gonna beat me and I won't let him do that, not anymore."

"But where will you go?" Rupert asked.

Timmy shrugged, slowing his packing for a second, thinking. Then he started again with renewed energy. "I'll go to Boston, that's where my grandma and grandpa live. I know they'll let me stay there."

Rupert took a step closer to Timmy. "But that's crazy; you're only a child, for the Creator's sakes. Boston is far away from here."

Timmy picked up his backpack and tossed it over his shoulder.

"That's not true, I'm old enough. I just need to get to where all the buses go to other places." He turned away from Rupert then and moved to the window. He slid it open, getting himself under the bottom frame. Once this task had been accomplished, he slid the screen up in its tracks, the window now open to the outside.

A cool breeze blew into his room, ruffling his hair with its passage. The smell of cut grass from a nearby home from earlier that evening still hovered in the air. Probably from his next door neighbor, he thought.

With one last look at Rupert, he started to climb out the window.

Rupert watched the small boy go, knowing what he was doing was crazy. Despite his best judgment, he couldn't let Timmy go out into the world alone. Knowing full well when he didn't return on this morning's portal he would be discovered, he decided he should go with the boy and keep an eye on him.

"Wait, Timmy. Can I come with you? I've never seen your world, with the exception of what I've seen on television. Maybe I could keep you company."

Timmy never hesitated, his eyes lighting up with the prospect of Rupert joining him.

"That would be great, Rupert," he said. Then his head swiveled to the bedroom door. David could be heard cursing in the hallway and his footsteps echoed across the quiet house.

Timmy knew it was now or never.

"Well, if you're coming, then come on," Timmy said, pulling his other leg through the window and dropping the three feet to the grass below. Rupert followed, sliding easily through the window. In less than three seconds later he was standing next to Timmy.

"Wow, how'd you do that?" Timmy asked, impressed.

Rupert shrugged, the gesture barely noticeable in the dark, plus all his fur masking only the more prominent body gestures.

"Magic."

"Cool," Timmy breathed. Then he repositioned his backpack to a more comfortable position and started out across his grass with Rupert by his side.

"You'll see, Rupert, once I get to my grandpa's house, he'll know what to do. Ever since my dad died I don't get to see them anymore. They used to come visit me and stay for a few days every now and then, but David won't let them, the big jerk!"

Rupert walked along beside him, listening to the boy. His own mind was swimming with what he was doing. The consequences, not to mention trying to keep Timmy safe, would be difficult.

If anyone was watching from a nearby house, they would have seen a small boy with a backpack walking down the sidewalk talking to himself in the middle of the night.

Timmy happily babbled on, content that for the first time in his short life, he was in control of his own destiny.

And once he made it to Boston and his grandparents, he knew everything would be all right.

Chapter Six

*I*T WAS JUST coming on one-thirty in the morning when Timmy made it to the bus station. He knew how to get there, as it was on his bus-route to school every morning.

Every morning he would drive past the bus station, watching all the buses with people on them; wondering where they were going and to what far away places all those people might be riding off to see.

But when he walked up to the first bus, he realized it might not be as easy as he thought. First of all, no one would believe an eight-year-old boy was out at two in the morning all alone, and second, he only had ten dollars to his name. He didn't know how much a bus ticket to Boston was, but he was pretty sure it was more than ten dollars.

The station was relatively silent, only a handful of other people waiting for one of the last few buses leaving that night. Inside the well-lit lobby, no one was able to see out to where Timmy had stopped, the boy still unobserved.

"What's wrong Timmy? We made it, didn't we?" Rupert asked.

Timmy sighed. "Yeah, we did, but I can't get on one of those buses. The second I do, someone's gonna stop me for being without a grown-up. We're stuck." He started to turn around and head back home, his head hanging low in defeat.

"This was a stupid idea. I should just go home and take what's coming to me. Maybe if I tell David I'm sorry it won't be so bad," he said, moving further away from the bus station.

Rupert didn't know what to do or say. He just stood there watching the small boy with the slumped shoulders as he moved away from him.

Then a voice from behind them made Timmy jump. "Hey there, son, are you okay, where's your parents?" An old man asked, a push broom in his hands.

Timmy was frozen in shock; he was caught before he had even begun! There were a few other people waiting for the next bus so Timmy decided to try something. Shaking off his surprise, he smiled at the old man.

"No, sir, I'm fine, my mom is in the bathroom. She told me to stay right here and not to move."

The old man nodded. "Those are good words to follow son, there's a lot of bad people out in the world that would want to do you harm." He nodded, agreeing with himself. "Well, you do what your mom said then and don't wander away. The next bus will be pulling out in a few minutes."

"Yes, sir, and thank you," Timmy said politely. The old man wandered away to return to work and Timmy breathed a sigh of relief

"Wow, that was close, I can't believe that worked. Maybe it's not too late. But I still don't know how we're gonna get on that bus."

Rupert kept trying to think of what they could do next and then his nose perked up as if he had just smelled something. His fur bristled along his back and he realized there was another monster in the immediate vicinity.

"Wait, Timmy, I think I might have an idea," Rupert said.

Timmy looked up at Rupert's face, his eyes wide with hope. "What?" he asked quietly.

Rupert's nose kept twitching and he started to move into the station. "Follow me, I smell another monster around. If I can find him, maybe he can help us."

Timmy ran up to walk at Rupert's side.

"What do you mean you smell another monster?"

Rupert's head was swiveling back and forth as he tried to figure out what direction to follow. "We monsters are sensitive to each other. Whenever we get too close to one another we can sense it. Usually that's not a problem, but now that I've left my assignment—namely your bedroom—it's possible to come across others."

Rupert moved between two buses, his nose twitching a little more. "This way," he pointed.

Timmy followed him, not really knowing what would happen when they found the other monster, but he knew he didn't want to go home, so anything that would delay the inevitable would be fine with him.

Rupert stopped at the back of a large Greyhound bus. There was a sign in the back window that said Boston, indicating the vehicle's destination. At the moment, no one was around, the bus waiting to be boarded by passengers in the station. Rupert moved to the side of the bus and opened a rear cargo door.

"All right, I know you're in there, so come on out. I just want to talk," Rupert said into the hollow luggage compartment. Timmy waited patiently, not really knowing what to expect. He jumped when a small monster as big as a medium-sized dog popped its head out.

The second Timmy saw it, he thought of the movie Gremlins, but only after the little cute guys had gotten wet and turned into hell-razing monsters. The creature had sharp claws and wore a baseball hat with the logo for the New York Yankees on its head. It frowned when it saw Rupert and Timmy. Moving to the edge of the compartment, it sat down on the edge, its skinny legs dangling an inch from the oil-soaked asphalt.

"Who are you and what are you doing here?" The gremlin asked.

Rupert turned to Timmy and placed a purple paw on his shoulder.

"This is my friend Timmy, he had to leave home in a hurry and now he's trying to get to Boston. I was hoping maybe you could help him out," Rupert said.

The gremlin scratched the side of his head. "Are you crazy? Hell, I could get disciplined for just talking to you. Aren't you supposed to be under someone's bed?"

"Umm, well yeah, about that. Something came up and now I'm with this child. So what do you say, can you help us out. I'd owe you one," Rupert said.

Timmy just stared at the gremlin, amazed. The gremlin noticed this and looked at Rupert. "What's his problem, hasn't he ever seen a gremlin before?"

"No, you're his first one," Rupert answered.

"Wow, this is so cool, so who do you scare here? I didn't know there were kids around here," Timmy gasped.

The gremlin hopped off the bus and stood in front of Timmy. "No kid, I don't scare children, I'm a gremlin; I mess stuff up." He walked around the boy as if he was sizing him up. "Let me put it this way. Did your mom ever hear a noise in her car and she couldn't figure out what it was from? That's me. That's what I do. I was about to catch a ride on this bus. I figured about halfway to its destination I was going to have it break down, that would really piss off the passengers."

"Could we come with you?" Timmy asked.

The gremlin shrugged. "Well, I'm kind of a solo act, but I tell you what. You take this bus and I'll find another." He turned to the luggage compartment. "Just crawl in there and move to the back. When the bus driver starts loading luggage, just be quiet. You should be fine."

"Hey, thanks, pal, you're all right," Rupert said with a smile, baring his fangs.

"Yeah, whatever. But listen, tall, dark and purple. What you're doing is so far off the mark that I wouldn't want to be you when the head monster finds out," the gremlin stated.

Timmy climbed into the luggage compartment, pushing his backpack in front of him. It was cold and dark and smelled like oil, but it would do in a pinch. Then he crawled back to the opening to wait for Rupert and listen to the two monsters talk.

Rupert frowned at the gremlin's words. "Yeah, I know, but I can't let the boy do this on his own. If he goes back home then what the head monster will do to me will be nothing compared to what the boy's father will do to him. He needs my help."

The gremlin's eyebrows went up a little. "Oh yeah? Father troubles, huh? Don't get me started about my dad. He was a bum." He turned and started to walk away. "Look, don't worry, your secret's safe with me, I won't say a word. Good luck," he said and with a wave walked around the bus to be lost from sight.

Rupert stood for another moment, his eyes scanning his surroundings.

"Come on, Rupert, are you coming inside or not?" Timmy asked from the edge of the luggage compartment.

Rupert climbed inside and Timmy slid forward and pulled the hatch down back to a closed position. The compartment was cast into darkness and the two of them sat quietly. Timmy curled up against him and Rupert wrapped his arms around the boy's small body.

Time passed and then voices could be heard coming from on the platform.

The compartment door was thrown open and luggage was tossed into the space. Timmy stayed in the far corner, the shadows keeping him invisible. Six or seven bags were tossed inside and then the hatch was closed once more.

The silence was broken as people boarded the bus, feet stomping overhead, and the vehicle shook as their bodies moved about in the passenger compartment overhead. Then the surge of the engine shook the walls of the luggage compartment. The engine was only a few feet away from Timmy and he felt his teeth vibrating from the idling motor.

After a few minutes crawled by, the engine surged and the bus started moving. Rupert and Timmy laid back and tried to get more comfortable. Neither of them had any idea how long they would be inside the luggage compartment, so both decided to just try to get as comfortable as possible and enjoy the ride.

The bus pulled out of the station and stopped at the red light at the corner with a hiss of air brakes. While the bus waited for the light to change from red to green, the driver changed the sign in the front and back window by punching in the name of the city he was going to on a small computer keypad on his dashboard. The digital name of Boston disappeared and a new name filled the sign.

New York, it said.

The light changed and the bus headed off to its new destination, the driver unaware of the stowaways he was carrying.

While inside the luggage compartment, Timmy had high hopes. He was on his way finally, and when the bus stopped, he would be in

Boston. Then he would call his grandparents and they would come and get him and everything would be okay.

The bus turned onto the highway and with a surge of the engine drove off into the night, its taillights soon disappearing into the darkness.

Chapter Seven

THE BUS ROCKED gently, the purring engine a continuous background drone. Conversation was hard in the confines of the luggage compartment so both Timmy and Rupert remained quiet.

Timmy fell asleep a little more than an hour after the bus had rolled out of the bus station. Rupert held the boy close, keeping him warm with his fur.

For the thousandth time since he had climbed into the luggage compartment with Timmy, he wondered what the hell he was doing. He was supposed to be under a bed or in a closet somewhere, not going on a journey in an unknown world.

Besides, there really wasn't much he could do to help the boy. He was intangible in his current form. True, he could touch Timmy, but that was only because he was his assigned child. To the rest of the populace of Timmy's world he was nothing more than a ghost or a wisp of smoke. Still, he was at least a voice of reason for the young boy, and once the boy made it to Boston, he could call his grandparents to pick him up and would be fine.

The bus hit a pot-hole in the highway, causing them to bounce around inside the compartment. Timmy stirred next to him, but remained sound asleep.

The hours passed and the roaring of the bus's engine slowed and then came to a dull idle, while the bus shook as people disembarked. The engine remained idling and Rupert crawled over the loose luggage to see where they were. Timmy lay on the floor, still sleeping.

Rupert peeked out of a small crack on the left side of the hatch where it had been bent from far too many times being slammed closed. His left eye squinted and he was able to make out a bus station similar to the one he and Timmy had recently left.

The sun was coming up, just a hint of scarlet on the horizon. He was only able to see a fraction of the sky thanks to his peephole, but it was enough.

A few humans milled around the bus, going in and out of the station. Fifteen minutes went by and the bus started bouncing as the passengers boarded again. The engine revved again and the bus started to move, the rest stop complete.

The bus drove onto the highway once again and the same engine droning filled the compartment once more.

Rupert went back to Timmy, lifting his head up and placing it back down onto his furry lap; the boy had remained asleep the entire time.

He sighed, thinking about what would happen next. This was all new to him. Until now, all Rupert had ever seen of Timmy's world was from the televisions he was able to spy from under the beds he'd occupied while on assignment. And the worst thing was, he needed to figure out just what he was supposed to do once Timmy found his grandparents. How would he find his way back to Monster City? He would have no way of knowing where any other monsters might be residing.

More time passed by uneventfully and these questions and more rattled around in his head until the bus slowed and finally stopped for the last time.

The luggage compartment door was opened and light flooded into the area. Rupert shook Timmy awake and the boy woke up, rubbing his eyes.

All of the luggage was removed and then the bus driver stopped cold with his head sticking into the compartment.

"What the hell? Hey, kid, what in the world are you doing in there?" The driver asked, scratching his head. "Get out of there," he ordered him.

Timmy sat up.

With daylight streaming into the compartment, he was now fully exposed. He grabbed his backpack and slowly crawled out onto the black tarmac.

The driver looked down at his little stowaway. "Well, are you going to answer me? Do your parents know where you are?"

That question had Timmy fully alert and scared. He looked up at Rupert, hoping his new friend would tell him what to do, but Rupert was stumped.

Timmy looked up at the bus driver. He had a kind face, so Timmy decided to tell him what he was doing.

"I'm going to Boston to see my Grandpa, but I didn't have enough money for a ticket, so I hid in there, I'm sorry, mister."

"Boston? Alone? Listen, son, you can't travel without parents or an adult guardian. I'm afraid you'll have to come with me to security. We can call your folks from there."

Timmy's eyes went wide. No! He thought, they couldn't do that! When David found him he didn't want to know what would happen to him. Deep inside his mind, all Timmy could think to do was run away, so he decided that was the perfect thing to do in this situation.

Taking a step backward, away from the bus driver, he turned and started running. "Come on, Rupert, let's get out of here!" He yelled, running as fast as his short legs would carry him.

"What the? Hey, kid wait, I won't hurt you! I just want to help!" The bus driver called, jogging a few feet after the boy, then deciding to give up. After all, it wasn't his fault the boy had snuck inside the luggage compartment, and if the kid ran away from him, then, so too, goes the evidence that he had done something wrong by letting a stowaway on board his vehicle.

Scratching his head, he closed the compartment door, wondering just who the hell was Rupert.

David walked down the dark hallway, heading to Timmy's room. It had taken almost ten minutes to calm Timmy's mother down. He had finally had to slip her another valium to shut her up. Now, while she lay sleeping in a drug induced haze, he opened the door to Timmy's room to take care of the little brat. He needed to silence the boy quickly. He knew what he did to the boy in the wee hours of the night was wrong, but he just couldn't help himself. He had been molested by his own father as a boy, and despite the fact that he had hated every second of it, he couldn't help but complete the circle and do the same to Timmy.

Now he knew if he didn't make sure the boy kept his secret, he would find himself going to jail.

And he knew what happened to men like him in jail.

Cringing at the thought, he stepped into Timmy's room. His eyes scanned the room in an instant, lastly falling onto the open window. He ran over to the window and stuck his head out of the opening, the cool night hair drying the sweat on his brow.

The boy was nowhere in sight.

With a few choice imprecations, he pushed away from the window and ran to the kitchen to grab his car keys. The brat couldn't have gone far.

After throwing on his overcoat, he ran to his car, and with a surge of life the engine raced. With a screech of tires, he backed out of the driveway and took off down the street, his mind trying to think of where an eight-year-old boy would go at two in the morning.

For the first hour he drove around in circles, not seeing the boy anywhere. Finally, he ended up at the bus station. Parking, he got out and went over to an old man sweeping debris around the inside of the station.

"Ah, excuse me, but I'm looking for my son. He's only eight and I think he might have run away from home. He didn't come by here by any chance, did he? He's got blonde hair and he's about so high," David said, holding his hand a little above his waist.

The old man stopped sweeping and leaned on his broom. His face wrinkled up until it looked like dried parchment more than a hundred years old. Then he smiled, showing the countless missing teeth in his mouth.

"Well, mister, I don't think I saw your boy tonight. There was only one child in here a little while ago and he said his momma was in the bathroom."

David frowned, thinking the odds of another boy being out this late at night in their small town was slim. So he decided to keep at the old man.

"But did you actually see the kid's parents?"

The old man thought on that, his face creasing until his eyes were just two small dots on his face. Then his face dropped back to being somewhat normal again.

"You know what? I didn't. Figured she was with him, and why not? It was almost two in the morning."

David grinned, hoping he had just got his first lead. "Listen, mister," he held out a twenty dollar bill to the old man, "you wouldn't know where that bus was headed now, would ya?"

The old man took the money, inspected it, and after it disappeared into his blue, baggy pants he pointed at the far wall where arrivals and departures were listed.

"Sure do, that bus went to New York."

David grinned and backed away from the man, already heading back to his car.

"Thanks, pal, thanks a lot," he said. Then he was around the corner, running to his car as fast as he could.

A minute later, with a screeching of tires, he pulled out of the bus station parking lot on his way to Route 95. He didn't know where the boy thought he was going, but he'd find him if it was the last thing he did.

He grinned as he pulled onto the highway. Timmy had no idea that he had just given David the perfect excuse to make the boy disappear for good once he found him.

When the police would ask him later, he would just play the sad and distraught step-father, heartbroken over his step-son's disappearance after he had run away from home.

He pressed on the gas pedal a little more, the car accelerating. When he found that boy he would make sure he never told another soul what had happened to him in the middle of the night.

David would make sure Timmy took his secret with him to the grave.

Chapter Eight

*T*IMMY RAN, NOT looking where he was going or where he'd been. After almost a full ten minutes of running, he slowed to catch his breath. At first he had been so preoccupied with running he hadn't given his surroundings much more then a glance, but now that he was stopped, he fully realized where he was and that he was lost.

The tall buildings loomed above him, making him feel like nothing more than an ant. People were everywhere, moving about on the sidewalk and the street, going to work or coming home from partying all night. Yellow taxi cabs were like swarming beetles, dozens of them for as far as his eyes could see. Cars honked and engines roared and he felt like he was in another world. He was struck by a passerby and he realized he was alone.

Rupert was nowhere to be seen.

"Rupert, are you there? Where are you?" He called out to the crowd of people.

A few strange and curious faces looked down at him as they passed him on the sidewalk, perhaps wondering what an eight-year-old boy was doing all alone on the streets of New York unattended, but no one cared enough to ask.

Timmy stood still, being struck in the shoulders again and again. He realized he needed to get out of the main path of walkers, so he moved to the alcove of a store. The store was closed, but the alcove served him well, keeping him away from all the pedestrians. On the cement, near his feet, were the remains of a cardboard box and a wine bottle, the residual house of a homeless person. Luckily, the owner was nowhere to be found.

Two black men walked over to him, their coats dirty, and as they moved closer, Timmy could smell the stench of alcohol coming off their bodies. He frantically looked around for Rupert, hoping to see his friend at any moment, but he was still nowhere to be seen.

"Well, well, well, look what we got here, Slim," one man said to the other. "Looks like someone lost a little white boy. What's your name, little cracker?"

Timmy stood quiet, too scared to say anything. Until this moment he hadn't been farther than the convenience store that was a few blocks away from his house back in Virginia.

"I'd say the little guy's plum scared shitless, Clarence," Slim said to his friend.

Slim reached into his pocket and pulled out a joint. It was about two inches long and was wound tight on both ends. Slim was proud of his work. The man slid the joint into his mouth and then pulled out a lighter. In one smooth motion, he lit the joint and then the lighter disappeared back into his coat like magic. He drew in a deep and then blew the acrid smoke into Timmy's face.

Timmy started to cough, causing Slim to chuckle. "Looks like the little guy can't hold his weed, man," Slim said to Clarence.

Clarence nodded, taking the glowing stick from his friend and taking a puff. While he held it in, the smoke filling his lungs, he nodded.

"Maybe we should take him back with us. Jerome might know what to do with him," Slim suggested.

Timmy tried to run then, but Slim caught him before he made it by him.

"Whoa there, little cracker; we're not done with you yet," Slim said, grabbing him by his backpack. Timmy was so scared he thought he might pee his pants. All the people that were walking by continued on, no one stopping to see what was happening.

No one cared.

"Leave me alone, please. My Mom'll be right back and she won't like you two talking to me," Timmy warned them.

Clarence let out his breath, smoke filling the small alcove they were occupying. "Mom, huh. I don't see no moms around here and I bet if she was true then she wouldn't leave her kid here all alone. No man, I think you be comin' with us."

Just then, an alabaster hand pushed between the two men.

"Excuse me, but just what do you think you're doing with my son? If you don't leave now, I'm going to scream in 1, 2…"

Before the woman could finish, Slim held up his hands in surrender. "Whoa, sweet momma, we were only messin' with the little guy, its cool. Ain't no need to call the law down here."

The woman smiled, but her eyes were hard. "Good, then go please." She stepped back so the two men could walk out onto the sidewalk, then they both took off down the street to be lost in the commotion of the busy city.

Timmy looked up at his savior, relief flooding through him.

"Thank you, ma'am, I didn't know what to do. I was so scared," Timmy said.

The woman bent over so her face was even with his. "That's okay, honey, I'm Susan, what's your name?"

"Timmy," he said bashfully."

"Well, hello, Timmy," she said then stood to her full height of five-six. "Timmy, where are your parents?"

Timmy looked up at her, not knowing what to say. A lie was forming in his mind, but when he looked into her eyes, his false bravado collapsed and he started crying.

"I ran away. I was trying to get to Boston to see my Grandpa, but the bus came here and now I don't know what to do and my friend Rupert was with me but we got separated and now I'm all alone," he rambled, tears rolling down his face.

Susan pulled him close. "There, there, honey, its okay. I tell you what, why don't we see if we can find Rupert and then we'll see about getting you home. Now what's Rupert look like?"

Timmy hesitated, but being only eight, he didn't see anything wrong with having a giant purple monster for a friend.

"Well, he's purple and he's a little taller than you. He's got claws on his hands and really sharp teeth, but he's friendly."

Susan looked down at Timmy, her face serious. "Timmy, is Rupert your imaginary friend?"

Timmy shook his head hard back and forth. "No way, he's my friend and he came with me from Virginia."

Susan nodded her head and then leaned down to be even with him again.

"Well, I tell you what, why don't I take you home with me and we'll try to find Rupert later? It's dangerous in the city and little boys aren't safe out here all alone."

Timmy bit his lip, while trying to make up his mind. He was alone and scared and this nice woman was offering to help him. He had no idea where Rupert was and he needed help.

He remembered learning at school the teacher saying if he was ever in trouble to tell an adult. He figured this would certainly count as one of those times. Finally, he nodded slowly, still hesitant, but not knowing what else to do. He sealed the deal when a large group of people walked by, yelling and cursing, followed by a smashed bottle that landed almost at Timmy's feet. He was so terrified he jumped into Susan's arms.

She smoothed his hair with her hand.

"That's okay, honey, you're safe now. I'll make sure no one hurts you." She turned and headed onto the sidewalk with Timmy's hand in hers. "My car is just around the corner, honey, and then I don't live too far away. Just over the bridge actually, we'll be there in no time."

With a few tears still on his cheeks, Timmy nodded and followed her. He felt safer now, not as scared. The people on the sidewalk that flowed by him moved aside just a little, the woman tall enough that she was more of an obstacle than a young boy. She brought him around the corner, the street looking much like the one he had just left. People were everywhere, some wearing fancy clothes and tuxedos. But some wore nothing but rags and pushed shopping carts full of stuff around in front of themselves. These people stopped by the overflowing trashcans and dug deep to find stuff; stuff that Timmy had no idea about. He saw one old woman pull what looked like a half eaten hotdog from a paper bag and devour it while she stood over the trashcan. Despite the disgusting sight, Timmy's stomach growled. He had just realized he hadn't eaten a thing since supper hours before and he was starving.

Eventually, they reached Susan's car and she opened the door and he slid inside. He turned to her and with a wan smile looked up into her face.

"Susan, is it possible I could get something to eat? I'm starving."

She rubbed his cheek with her thumb, wiping away a stray tear.

"Of course, honey, once we get home." Then she started the car and pulled out into the street, cutting a cab off and flipping the driver the finger when he cursed at her.

Timmy laid back against the seat, buckling his seatbelt when she pointed to it. They headed out of the city and over a giant bridge that had Timmy's mouth falling open, and the tall buildings of the city faded away behind the car. Without realizing it, Timmy drifted off into a light sleep, the adrenalin rush of the past hour disappearing, hitting him hard. His head drooped against the passenger window and Susan turned to look at him and smiled sweetly.

But then her face grew hard, all business. She reached into her coat for her cell phone and hit a few buttons. A moment later her call was answered.

"Yeah, what is it, I'm in the middle of something," a deep male voice said.

"Well, get unbusy, because I have something for you," Susan said into the phone.

"Oh, really, may I ask what it is?" The voice asked, intrigued.

"Really, Charlie, don't be coy, you know exactly what it is. I've been out on the streets all night looking for just the right candidate." She looked down at the peaceful face of Timmy and grinned malevolently, the rising sun flashing across her eyes and giving her a demonic countenance. "I was just about to give up and come back home when I got lucky. He literally fell into my lap."

"Oh, really, I'm listening," the male voice said.

"Not yet, dear. You'll have to wait until I get there. But I've got another one for you. See you soon."

Without waiting for an answer, she snapped the cell phone shut and concentrated on driving, the same demonic look plastered on her face.

Soon the fun would begin.

CHAPTER NINE

*R*UPERT WATCHED TIMMY run away from him and the bus driver. He wasn't quite sure what was happening, and by the time he figured it all out, Timmy had turned the corner and was gone from sight.

Rupert realized he needed to go after the boy before he lost him. He took off at a run, his furry body grazing the bus driver. The man held his hand to his face, feeling the breeze of Rupert's passing. With the exception of Timmy, to all others he was nothing more than an ephemeral being; a slight breeze as he passed them by.

The driver held his hand to his face for a moment longer, a chill running down his spine, then he shook it off and returned to the bus. He had a little over an hour layover and then it was on to Boston to finish his route. He figured he'd grab a burger and a cup of coffee before returning back to the bus to fill out some paperwork. The driver moved away, never knowing how close he'd come to witnessing an actual monster from another dimension.

Rupert jogged to the street corner he had seen Timmy disappear around, his eyes trying to see everywhere at once. There were people everywhere, walking, running, arguing. The city was incredible, the smells and sounds almost overwhelming to his sensitive senses. The extra time it was taking for Rupert to find Timmy's spore was valuable time he didn't have to spare.

He started moving down the street, people moving around him as if they sensed he was there but didn't quite realize it.

But that was exactly what was happening.

On some unconscious level, all humans sensed him, but barely realized it. This manifested itself by people quickly avoiding whatever space he occupied. He moved down the sidewalk, calling Timmy's name, but the boy was nowhere to be found. His nostrils flared as he picked up the subtle trace of the boy. After spending so much time with Timmy, Rupert had memorized the child's scent.

Moving off down the sidewalk, he followed the trail, like he was following the scent of a fresh baked apple pie sitting on a windowsill on a summer's day.

He made it to a small alcove and stopped. The scent was strong here and he quickly followed it back onto the street and around the next corner.

Just as he turned the corner, he saw Timmy getting into a car with a strange woman. He called out to him, but he was too far away for the boy to hear him.

Then it was too late, the car pulling out into traffic and disappearing around another street corner.

Rupert stood there, helpless. He had no idea what to do next. The boy he had taken responsibility for was driving away in a strange car and he had no idea how to catch up to him.

He leaned against a wall of a copy store and sulked.

"Hey, pal, what's wrong?" A disembodied voice asked.

Rupert looked up, not realizing the voice was talking to him.

"Yeah that's right, big, dumb and purple. I'm talking to you."

Rupert looked around him, trying to discern where the voice was coming from, until the voice helped him out.

"Psst, hey, I'm down here," said the voice from a sewer opening next to the sidewalk.

Rupert crawled over to the grate and knelt down on all fours. The smell coming from the sewer made the odors above ground almost sweet in comparison. He winced and pulled back his head.

"Wow, that stinks," Rupert said with a sour look on his furry face.

"Hey, thanks a lot, that's my home you're insulting," the voice snapped back.

Rupert regained some of his composure and leaned back towards the grate.

"I'm sorry, but all this is new to me."

"Oh yeah? Why, what are you, one of those guys who get's the cushy inside jobs in a closet or under a bed?" The voice asked.

Rupert nodded, slowly. "Yes, I'm afraid I am. I'm sorry if that bothers you."

"Ah, its okay, I'm just a little jealous and I'm not afraid to admit that. It's not so bad down here, though. I mean, I get all the rats I can eat, it's a friggin' buffet down here."

Rupert made a face again. "Delightful," he said.

"Yeah, well, listen, pal, I saw you chasing that kid and I thought I could help."

Rupert leaned a little closer to the grate. All he could see were two small, red eyes and a row of very sharp teeth.

"Oh, really, just help, no strings attached?" Rupert asked. He was desperate, but he had never known or heard of a sewer monster doing anything if there wasn't something in it for them.

Almost as if the sewer monster was prepared for Rupert's question, the monster smiled, razor-sharp teeth flashing in the wan light filtering into the sewer.

"Well, maybe I might want something."

"Ah-hah, I knew it!" Rupert said, backing away from the grate.

"Now, wait a sec, hear me out, will ya."

Rupert stopped, he was desperate after all.

"Listen, I've got some pals in the grapevine, we've got the sewers wired from here to Jersey. If that kid is around, I'll hear about it." He hesitated for a moment for dramatic effect and then said: "So are you interested or should I take my business elsewhere?"

"No wait, I'm interested. So what do you want in return?" Rupert asked.

The creature shrugged, his eyes jumping slightly in the grate. "Not much; just put in a good word for me when you get back to Monster City. The names Rocky."

A scaly green hand slipped out of the hole under the curb and Rupert shook it. Rupert then had to wipe his hand on the sidewalk to remove the green slime Rocky's handshake had left there.

"Okay, Rocky, you got yourself a deal. I'm Rupert, by the way."

"Rupert? What kind of a name is that? Jeez, pal, maybe you should go hang out with the fairies in Central Park."

Rupert frowned. He'd heard how rude New York monsters could be, but he had no idea exactly just how rude.

"Yeah, well, I'm named after my grandfather and if you don't like it, that's tough for you!" Rupert snarled back, baring his fangs.

"Whoa, hey, easy there, champ; I was just kidding. You know, it gets kind of boring down here. I only get to have a little fun when the DPW comes down here. Man the fun I have."

"Whatever," Rupert said, not really interested in hearing his tales of frightening the city workers of New York City.

"So how will I get in touch with you if you hear something?" Rupert asked, changing the subject as he was not very interested in Rocky's business.

Rocky pointed his hand out of the grate, one clawed finger pointing down the road. "Go that way, towards Central Park. I might have been joking, but it's a good place to eat. When I find something out, I'll tell one of the fairies and she'll find you. Until then, get a slice of pizza and relax. They make a good pie over on 22nd Street, go there."

Rupert nodded, thanked Rocky and then stood up, pedestrians flowing around him like he was a large boulder in the middle of a river. He started up the street, careful to avoid all the pedestrians. When he passed through a human, he received a weird tingling sensation for his troubles, so he did his best to avoid people at all costs.

The noise, the sound and the lights were unbearable and he wondered how humans managed to stay sane in all this chaos.

Crossing the street unscathed, he headed off for Central Park. No matter how anxious he was to find Timmy, he had to be patient and wait. Thanking the Creator he'd found Rocky, or better yet, that

Rocky had found him, he moved off deeper into the city and sent a silent prayer to Timmy to just be all right for a little while longer.

David pulled over at the bus station in New York City. After a few times around the block, he was lucky enough to find a parking spot. Jumping out of the car, he went over to the bus terminal. The smell of diesel fumes filled the area, causing him to hold his breath. Once he was through the worst of it, he started looking at the signs on the buses.

He questioned driver after driver and then went inside to the ticket counter to see if Timmy had gone inside the station.

No luck, but he wasn't ready to give up just yet.

After he'd checked all the buses in the terminal, he saw that the ninth bus said Boston on the front windshield. He remembered what Timmy had said about his grandfather and wondered if the boy would have been crazy enough to try to make it all the way to Boston.

That's when another bus driver came around from the back of the bus. David hadn't talked to this man yet and waited as the driver came close to him. He had a cup of coffee in his hand and a newspaper, and he whistled softly while he walked through the maze of buses as he headed directly toward David.

David waited, figuring after asking this driver if he'd seen Timmy, he'd be out of luck.

"Excuse me, but I was looking for my son. I was wondering if you might have seen him last night; or maybe this morning," he said, looking at his watch and seeing it was going on almost seven in the morning. He had driven all night to reach New York and now had come the impossible task of finding one small boy in a city of millions.

"Oh, yeah, what did this boy look like?" The bus driver asked.

David leaned against the bus on his right, casually. "He's got blonde hair and is about eight years old. Look, mister, he ran away from home and I'm just trying to find him."

The driver's eyebrows went up. "No kiddin'? Well, you're sort of in luck. When I pulled into the terminal this morning there was a boy fitting that description hiding in my luggage compartment. But when I told him I had to bring him to security, he took off. He was fast, too.

He'd made it around the corner and was gone before I barely knew it. Sorry I can't be of more help."

David was shocked, he was incredibly lucky to have caught a scent of Timmy's trail. In fact, if his luck held, he should make sure to play the lottery as he was one of the luckiest people in the city right now.

David shook the man's hand. "No, really that's fine. At least I know he made it here in one piece, thanks." David turned to leave when the bus driver called him back.

"Hey, wait a sec'. There was one other thing the boy said. When I asked him where he was going, he said he was going to see his grandfather in Boston. Crazy, huh?"

David smiled back. "Yeah, crazy. Well, thanks a lot," David said, waving as he walked away.

The driver waved back. "Sure, good luck. He seemed like a cute kid, wouldn't want anything bad to happen to him; that would be a shame."

David smiled at that, but the smile was thin and false. "Yeah, I know what you mean, that would be a shame." Then he headed back to his car.

Boston was hours away, and if Timmy had managed to get on another bus, then he already had a good head start.

Pulling back onto the busy street, he grinned to himself. He had beaten the odds and had found the boy, perhaps God wanted him to succeed.

Leaning back in his seat, he turned on the radio and enjoyed the beautiful day.

A song he liked came on the radio and he started to sing, his off-key voice filling the vehicle and overriding the music.

He would find the boy and shut him up and everything would be fine.

CHAPTER TEN

*T*IMMY AWOKE TO the sound of the car stopping. The sun was high in the sky; casting its brilliance across the quaint suburban street. He blinked his eyes a few times, trying to gain his bearings, then he heard his car door open and he looked up into the face of Susan.

A few wisps of her dark-blonde hair had fallen over her face, giving her an angelic quality as the light from the sun cast her in a soft glow.

He blinked again and the glow was gone, only to be replaced by the woman's smile.

"We're here, honey, why don't you hop out and we'll go inside. It's been a long night for both of us, I'm sure."

He nodded, and with a grin, stepped out of the car. The street he was on was a neat suburb that could be anywhere on the east coast. Cars lined the sidewalk and were in driveways, while newspapers sat on front walkways, waiting for their owners to retrieve them. Dogs barked from backyards, waiting to be let back inside after finishing their business and a pretty woman with brown hair jogged by with her baby in a stroller, the baby carriage looking more like some futuristic tripod than a stroller.

Blinking the sleep from his eyes, and stretching sore muscles, he followed her inside the one-story, brown house. Flowers lined the walkway and a statue of a gnome stood quietly on the lawn overlooking the entire neighborhood.

A sticker for PETA was in the front window, the occupants of the house proclaiming to everyone their opinions on the subject of fur.

With Susan in the lead, she opened the front door and the two entered the house, Susan placing her keys back in her pocket once they stepped inside the small foyer.

She looked down at Timmy. "I've got a surprise for you," she said softly.

Timmy looked up at her, not understanding. Everything was moving so quickly he barely had a chance to catch his breath.

"Can I call my Grandpa, now?" He asked nicely.

He hoped he could look up the name in a phone book as he didn't know the phone number from memory.

She patted his head gently. "Later, dear, but right now why don't we get you something to eat and then you can go to bed and get some real rest. Hmm?"

Timmy yawned, realizing he was still tired. She grinned and started walking into the kitchen. It was a bright kitchen filled with pictures of sunflowers everywhere as a theme. The door handles on the cabinets were all little sculpted flowers and the border of the wall, near the ceiling, was a painted molding of different size sunflowers.

Timmy was no decorator, but it all seemed a little too bright, but then he was a boy and wasn't too much for flowers.

Susan made him some toast and peanut butter and he inhaled it greedily, his stomach now a live thing that needed to be fed. After that, she gave him a bowl of cereal. He wasn't sure, as he hadn't seen the box, but he was pretty sure it was Fruity Pebbles. He ate it hungrily, and once finished, sat back in the chair, sighing.

"Thank you, Susan; that was great."

"Your welcome, honey." She placed a small glass of orange juice on the table in front of him and smiled.

"Now just drink your juice and you'll be ready to get some rest."

He looked up at her face, not seeing any reason not to think she wasn't what she pretended to be. He drank the orange juice in a few gulps, wincing at the tiny after taste. It tasted a little sour, but that could have just been the brand.

He placed the cup back on the table.

"Thanks again, Susan; that was great. Now can I call my Grandpa?"

She stood over him, not saying anything. He thought that was odd and was about to ask her what was wrong when he suddenly felt his eyes drooping. He rubbed them, not realizing why he was so tired all of a sudden. He reached out to her with his left hand, wanting to get her attention, but his arm barely moved before flopping back down to his side. His limbs felt heavy and he realized he couldn't keep his eyes open. Not understanding he had just been drugged, he closed his eyes and was prepared to take a nap on the kitchen table until Susan caught his slouching body and picked him up. He wasn't heavy and she easily carried him out of the kitchen and down a small hallway.

Multiple doors lined the hall, each with a padlock on the outside. She opened one and carried Timmy inside. Once the door was closed behind her, she took off his sneakers and laid him gently down on the small twin bed. The Spiderman sheets were pulled back and Timmy was tucked in. He rolled over in his drug induced sleep, breathing heavier. Susan backed away from him, looking down on him like a mother to a son. Then she left the room, making sure to padlock the door once it was closed.

She detoured by the bathroom, washing her face and freshening up. Once her minor chores were finished and she felt a little more refreshed, she walked down the small hallway again, this time moving to the last door on the left. She opened it slowly, not wanting to startle the occupants, although she knew they were still sleeping.

They had been up late last night and she expected them to sleep for at least another hour. With her head peeking into the room, she scanned the two small twin beds closely. Two children were sleeping softly, one in each bed, ages around nine or ten; they never heard her come in.

Their chest's rose and fell gently as they slept off the nights exertions.

The boy and girl now occupying the beds had been with her for almost a month now and they behaved very well. But it hadn't been that way at first, but lack of sleep and food had soon had them aching to please her and her husband.

A few slaps in the face had helped, as well.

Thinking of Charlie, she locked the bedroom door and moved off to another side door in the short hallway and slipped inside. Her husband was sitting at a desk, working over something. As she moved closer, she realized it was a script. He liked to write the scripts to their little movies, although she found it irrelevant. Still, he was her husband and she loved him, so was willing to let him have his fun if he enjoyed it. On the end of the desk was a pile of work orders. He looked up as she entered and just nodded in her direction.

"It's about time you got back, I was beginning to get worried."

She sat down in a chair next to him and waved his question away.

"Why, you know I always get the best ones early in the morning. By then they've spent a long night on the streets and are always eager to come with me. Nothing's changed."

"So, you have a surprise for me? Is the child young? Boy or girl?"

She leaned forward as if she was telling him a secret. "Boy; and he can't be a day over eight, if I'm right."

Charlie's teeth gleamed in the light of the room. "Excellent, in fact, he's just what we need. Some of our subscribers were just saying we needed to get some new actors."

She leaned back in her chair, checking one of her nails to see if she had broken it. "Well, there you go then, problem solved."

"When do you want to integrate him into the movie with the others?" Charlie asked, his eyes flashing with excitement.

"Soon, let's give him some time to get acclimated to his new surroundings. We'll have him start by just watching and then we'll work him into it slowly." She flashed him an evil grin. "You'll see, I have a feeling he'll be our best one yet." Then she stood up, kissed her husband on the cheek and left the room. She was tired and thought after she'd taken a shower, she would take a nap, as well.

As she walked down the small hallway, she passed by an open closet door. She stopped here and frowned, looking inside it. Charlie knew better then to leave this door open. It was just careless.

Reaching inside, she saw the false back was open, also. Inside were dozens of DVD's, each labeled neatly in black print. Each DVD had a child's name on it, some with stars next to their names to show how much better they had been than others. She slid the false wall back in place, telling herself she'd have to make sure to chastise Charlie about it later. They needed to always be on guard, and leaving the closet open was just carelessness. She closed the false back and shut the closet door. Then, satisfied all was in order, she headed off to the bathroom to take a much needed shower.

CHAPTER ELEVEN

AT THE SAME time Susan was escorting Timmy out of her car and up the path to her house, another monster was watching.

On Susan's lawn, the gnome's head swiveled ever so slightly. He watched her go up the path and then disappear into the house. He had already heard that one of their own was looking for a human child. He knew Susan had no children of her own, despite the fact that she continuously brought different kids back to the house

The funny thing was, the gnome never saw the kids leave.

A dog came walking up the sidewalk, the owner far behind the animal. The dog took one look at the gnome and wandered onto the grass.

The gnome's face crunched up in anger, but it knew it couldn't move on the off chance the human would see.

The dog started sniffing and he tried to shoo it away.

"Psst, get out of here, don't you do what I think you're gonna do," the gnome said to the animal. The dog grunted, not quite sure what to make of a talking statue.

"Scram, beat it, so help me if you do it, I'll find you," the gnome growled softly. Then the human was too close to him and he had to stay perfectly still.

"Come on, Dusty, do your business so I can go home," the dog's owner said in a bored voice.

The dog sniffed a few more times, lifted its leg and then peed all over the side of the gnome. Finished, it trotted away, happy it had marked its territory in a new place.

The gnome made a disgusted face, and looked down at himself.

"Great, I just had this suit cleaned." Then it made sure the area was clear and slipped away into the bushes. There was another monster living under the porch, a giant slug-like creature, and the gnome knew he could pass on the information he had. The slug would make sure to get the info to the right creatures, who would then pass it along all the way back to New York.

Smelling like urine, the gnome moved into the shrubs, already planning on washing up in the bird bath after he was finished talking with the slug.

*   *   *

Rupert sat on a park bench on the outskirts of Central Park. No one occupied the bench with him, and in fact on the few occasions someone did sit down next to him, they would only stay for a few moments, then feeling uncomfortable for no apparent reason, they would move to another bench.

Rupert barely noticed.

He watched a flock of pigeons being fed by an old man. The old man was throwing pieces of bread from a paper bag onto the gravel path. The birds were ravenous, feeding on the bread before it could come to rest on the path.

Rupert let out a deep, frustrated sigh.

All he could do was wait and he had never been much of a waiter.

Time passed and the sun rose higher in the sky. Despite his agitation, he found he had drifted off into a light nap and it was only the feeling of something pulling on his fur that brought him out of his daydream.

He cracked his eyelids and glanced down to see a fairy gently tugging his purple fur. He opened his eyes fully and with a yawn, tried to smile.

"Yes, can I help you?" He asked.

"The question is more like, can I help you," the fairy said. "The names Rhonda." She was about five inches tall and was wearing a pair of jeans and a t-shirt that read: Born Beautiful.

Rupert sat a little taller, stretching his limbs. Muscles rippled under his purple fur, but the fairy never noticed, and if she did, she did an excellent job of hiding it.

"Oh, really," he said, while gazing down at her, taking in her clothes. "Tell me; is that the formal uniform for fairies in the city now?"

She looked down at her clothes and set her face in a tight grimace.

"What's the matter with my clothes? What are you, the fashion police? Listen, I heard something about that kid you were looking for. You want the information or what," she snapped.

That had Rupert's attention and he sat up ramrod straight. The fairy backed up a little, not wanting to be too close to those large feet, her wings fluttered for a moment, and then remained still.

"Have you heard something? Is he all right? Where is he?"

"Whoa, slow down there, big guy. Rocky said you got an 'in' with the head monster, so in exchange for the info, I need you to put in a good word for me, too. Do you know what it's like having to live in this park all the time? Day after day and month after month. I need a change of scenery, something inside, maybe."

Rupert nodded quickly. "Sure, sure, fine, whatever you want, just tell me where the boy is."

The fairy flew up and landed on his shoulder. "He's in Jersey; the suburbs actually. We got a gnome on the inside. He spotted him earlier and passed it through the grapevine."

Rupert stood up, anxious to move, but not knowing what to do.

"That's great, but how do I get to him? I mean, it's not like I can just call a cab and take that to New Jersey."

The fairy left his shoulder and fluttered by his face. "Ah, but that's where you're wrong, my big, purple friend." A pigeon flew near her and tried to peck her. She swatted it with her wand and the bird retreated.

"Filthy beasts, for some reason they can see me and they think I'm a snack. Just one more reason I want out of here. Come on, follow me." She started flying out of the park, heading toward the street. She turned once to make sure Rupert was following her and then continued on her way.

Rupert moved as fast as he could, trying to keep the small fluttering object of the fairy in sight. Soon she had reached the edge of the park, the busy street filled with cars and bicycles and taxi cabs; she stopped.

Rupert caught up to her and she pointed to a cab stand across the street.

"See those cabs over there?" Rhonda asked.

Rupert nodded.

"Okay, what I want you to do is go over there and wait for one to pull in line. When you find one that has no driver, get in. Then wait for me to do my stuff."

"Yeah, but what about…"

Rhonda cut him off. "Relax, big and purple, I know what I'm doing. Just do what I say and you'll be on your way in no time."

Rupert sighed, hardly believing he was leaving his destiny to a fairy, but what other choice did he have?

Weaving around the cars in the street, he made it to the other side easily. He actually didn't know what would happen if he was struck by a car. He may have been ephemeral, but for all he knew he could get stuck or fused into one of the vehicles. All in all it was better to just avoid them.

He waited for a cabby on the end of the line to leave his vehicle to get a cup of coffee. Rupert took the time to slide into the open window of the cab, his fur rubbing the sides of the window frame.

He waited patiently, wondering what would happen next. He found out when he saw Rhonda fly over to the cabby and perch herself on his shoulder. She started whispering into his ear and waving at the cab. The cabby listened, not even realizing he was hearing her.

Then the cabby turned away from the newspaper stand he was standing in front of and walked back to his cab. He climbed in and started the cab, with a large cloud of exhaust smoke bellowing out of the exhaust.

Rhonda flew into the back seat of the cab and sat on the passenger's head rest, smiling at Rupert and swinging her legs back and forth like a child on a swing.

"What did you do to him, why'd he come back?" Rupert asked, perplexed.

She smiled. "I just whispered into his ear that he should take a ride to New Jersey. By the time the suggestion wears off you should be close to where you need to be, so pay attention. When he starts to look around like he doesn't know where he is, and he has no idea how he made it to Jersey, then it's time for you to leave the cab."

The cab pulled out into the street, cutting off three other motorists as the vehicle moved into the right lane. Beeping horns and screeching tires added to the rest of the cacophony of the big city.

Rhonda took flight then, and with a quick wave, flew out the window.

"Don't forget, you promised to put in a good word for me." Then she was gone.

Rupert watched the streets blur by as the cabby worked his way out of the city. He sat back in the seat, his fur blowing in the wind coming in through the window. Whatever would happen next, at least he was on his way to find Timmy.

Chapter Twelve

*T*IMMY WOKE UP suddenly, not knowing where he was.

He looked around the room he was in, for just a moment thinking he was still home, safe in his own bed. Then everything that had happened in the past twelve hours came flooding back to him. He looked down at the bed he was lying in. Spiderman bed sheets covered him, and as he looked around at the walls, he realized he was in a child's room.

Stuffed animals lined the far wall and an Xbox sat on the floor in front of a nineteen-inch television. He got out of bed and felt a pressure on his bladder, which needed to be addressed immediately.

Walking to the bedroom door, he opened it halfway. He looked out onto a small hallway with numerous other doors, all closed. He had no way of knowing that Susan had unlocked the door to check on him only an hour earlier and had forgotten to relock it after being distracted by Charlie.

Stepping into the hallway, he moved quietly down the middle, careful not to make a sound. He remembered the nice woman who had helped him and knew he was in her house, but for the life of him couldn't remember when he had fallen asleep. He wondered about Rupert, too. He had become separated from his friend and had no idea how to find him.

He slowed at the end of the hall, the door there slightly ajar. Stepping closer, he pushed it open to discover it was the bathroom he so sorely needed.

Stepping inside, he used the toilet and then got a drink of water from the faucet, using a Dixie cup from a stack sitting on the end of the sink. He drank three cups, not understanding why he was so thirsty. He had no way of knowing the drug that had knocked him out earlier that morning had a side effect of leaving a person with dry-mouth.

Looking around the bathroom, he saw nothing out of the ordinary. A can of shaving cream sat on the end of the sink and a book of matches were perched on the shelf above the toilet.

He knew not to touch matches, that they were dangerous. He remembered his real father had kept a book of matches in the bathroom and whenever he had gone number 2, he'd always lit one after he left the bathroom.

Timmy never understood what that meant. He could still smell his father's odor and then on top of it he had to smell the sulfur from the matches. All together it smelled worse than if his dad had just gone to the bathroom and left the room like it was.

He washed his hands and had one more cup of water.

When his thirst was quenched, he stepped back into the hallway. He could hear voices coming from one of the distant rooms and he decided that would be as good a place as any to go. Walking back towards his bedroom, he stopped at the closest door. Turning the doorknob, he opened it and peeked inside.

His mouth fell open when he saw the interior of the room.

There were toys everywhere. Trains, action figures and dolls lined the voluminous shelves in the room. Then his eyes stopped at the two children in the middle of the floor. There was a boy and a girl standing close together, hugging. Timmy didn't give their activities much thought, but was pleased to see other children and so stepped into the room. That's when he saw a man and Susan in the room, also. They were all the way in the corner and the man was standing in front of a tripod with a camcorder on it. Next to him was a television monitor, but from where Timmy stood at the door, he couldn't see what was on it.

The man looked up at Timmy's entrance and smiled. "Well, well. Look who's up. Come on in here, young man, and meet the family," he said with a smile. Then he turned to Susan.

"Stupid bitch, you forgot to lock his door," he whispered angrily.

She ignored him and walked over to Timmy and held out her hand. "Hi, Timmy, how are you feeling? Better I hope."

Timmy shrugged. He was still a little groggy but otherwise felt fine.

"I'm okay, I guess. Can I call my grandpa now? Maybe he could come and get me if I tell him where I am," Timmy said. He was starting to realize running away had probably been a bad idea and he really just wanted to go home. At the moment, dealing with his step-father was the last thing on his mind.

Susan smiled down at him. "I'm sorry, honey, but you can't do that. At least not right now. Maybe in a few days. Until then why don't you stay and play with us."

She pointed to the boy and girl, who were no longer hugging. "You can play with Mark and Janice. Would you like that?"

Timmy just shrugged. He wanted to go home, but Susan was just so nice. "Well, I guess I could stay for a little while." His eyes glanced over at the Transformer action figures and Star Wars toys sitting on one of the shelves. "Can I play with those toys?"

Susan backed away from him and gestured to the toys. "Of course, go right ahead. Mark and Janice are playing a different game. Maybe you could watch for a while and when you're ready, maybe you could play with them, too?" She asked sweetly.

Timmy ran over to the toys, barely hearing her. "Sure, yeah, I guess so," he said, already pulling down a Boba Fett and a Han Solo action figure. There were ships, too, to put the figures in and he was lost in all the scenes he could act out from the movies. He only had a few Star Wars toys at home, David saying they were stupid and not letting his mother buy him anymore than what he already owned.

He sat on the floor playing with the toys, not really seeing what else was happening in the room. Across the room, though, Charlie got the other two children to go back to hugging. Susan stood near them, as well, although not so close that she got into the picture.

Susan had the two children take off their shirts and lay down together. She coached Mark how to kiss Janice on the cheek and lips, the boy doing what he was told like he was in a trance.

At first, Timmy didn't notice what was happening, engrossed in the toys, but slowly he started looking over to the two children. From where he sat on the floor, he could also see the television monitor. The screen showed the two children doing stuff that Timmy thought was gross, that only his mom and dad did in their bedroom when he was sleeping. He remembered one time just before his father had died; he had gotten up real early, having to use the bathroom. His parent's door had been open a little and he had heard sounds, his mother sounding like she was moaning in pain. He had crept over to the door and had seen his daddy on top of his mommy. At first he had thought he was hurting her, but after a few minutes he realized his mom was happy and seemed to be enjoying it. In fact she seemed to be praying, because every few seconds she would yell: "Oh God, oh God."

He had snuck back to his room and when he was in school later that morning he had asked Rudy Gibbons if he had known what his parents had been doing. Rudy had told him that they were having S...E...X and that was how babies were made. Timmy hadn't believed him and had forgotten about the entire thing…at least until right now when he saw the two kids doing the same thing.

He stopped playing and watched, thinking it was gross and yet idly curious. Susan saw him watching and walked over to him.

"Would you like to come and play with them? Look at how much fun they're having. And when we're all done, we're all going to go into the kitchen and have some ice cream." She bent at the waist until her face was only a few inches from Timmy's. "So what do you say, do you want to play with us?"

Timmy shook his head no. Whatever they were doing, he knew kids weren't supposed to do it. His teacher had told his entire class in school one day after recess.

Timmy stood up and backed away from her. "No, thank you, I don't want to play. I think I changed my mind. I want to call my mom right now."

Susan moved closer to him, Timmy stopping when his back came up against a shelf full of toys. With her smile never faltering from her lips, she looked down at him. Behind her, Charlie had stopped filming and the other two kids were now watching with mild interest.

"I'm sorry you don't want to play with us, but I'm afraid you have to. I really need you to come over here now. I promise you'll like it. Then we'll get ice cream," she said gently with just a touch of impatience in her voice.

Timmy shook his head, his heart starting to beat faster. He felt trapped and he knew what he did and didn't want to do. And he didn't want to join Mark and Janice.

"No! I don't want to and you can't make me," he said back sharply.

Susan's smile vanished like smoke in the wind. She took a step closer to Timmy, her hand reaching out to grab his arm. Timmy cried out from surprise and pain.

"Now, you listen to me, you little shit! I say what you do and don't do around here and you'll join Mark and Janice whether you like it or not!" Her nostrils flared and spittle left her lips in anger.

Timmy had been taught he was supposed to respect adults, but he knew something wasn't right.

"No I won't!" He screamed and then he kicked Susan in the leg. Now she cried out in pain and surprise, bending over and rubbing her leg. As she did this, she let Timmy's arm go. Timmy took advantage of it and ran to the only door in the room.

Opening it wide, he dashed into the small hallway, running as fast as he could to the end where it opened up into a modest living room. He darted across the room, and upon reaching the door he thought would lead to the outside world, he tried to open it.

It was locked from the inside, a deadbolt lock that could only be opened with a key. He ran to one of the closest windows, and when he pulled the curtains aside, saw there were steel bars on the windows. From the outside, the bars would just look like the homeowners were just worried about being robbed, the metal twisted into ornate designs.

Timmy backed away from the window, feeling very trapped. He saw a phone on the table and ran to it. He was about to pick it up when he saw it had a padlock on it. Without the key, he couldn't pick up the receiver.

Footsteps made him turn around to see Susan and Charlie standing in the doorframe calmly. Charlie's face was a mask of indifference, but Susan's face was red with anger from her sore leg. Charlie folded his arms over his chest and smiled at Timmy from across the room.

"Happy now?" Charlie asked. "There's no way out." He held up a set of keys and jingled them in front of his chest. "These are the only way out of here and I don't think I'll be giving them to you. Now be a good boy and come back in the room with us. Don't make this any harder on yourself then you have to."

Timmy backed away to the side, seeing the kitchen. Maybe there was a way out that way. Tensing his legs, he moved as close as he could to them and then ran into the kitchen, surprised to see neither of the grown-ups following him. He tried the back door, but it was locked the same as the front door.

His eyes looked everywhere at once trying to find a way to escape. Charlie and Susan moved to the opening that separated the living room from the kitchen. Timmy saw another door in the middle of the interior kitchen wall and ran to it. His heart filled with relief when he turned the doorknob and the door opened.

He was greeted to a set of stairs leading downward and a blackness as dark as night. With nothing to lose, he charged down the stairs, hoping he didn't slip and fall, but too scared to really care. Reaching the bottom, he turned to see the silhouette of Charlie and Susan at the top of the basement stairs.

They just stood there, not following him down into the cellar. His pulse pounded in his temple and his breathing came quick as he stood there. He continued backing up, not knowing where he was going, but every inch he was farther away from the two adults the better.

The heel of his sneaker struck something and he fell over backward, not having enough time to so much as let out a surprised gasp.

His fall was broken by something soft, and the crinkling sound of plastic bags came to his ears. He flailed around in whatever he'd fallen into, desperately trying to get back up, but the plastic was slippery and he couldn't find purchase.

It felt like he was drowning without the water.

Then footsteps drifted down the stairs over the sounds of the rustling plastic and he looked up to see Charlie and Susan coming for him.

That's when Charlie reached out with a hand and flicked the light switch on the basement wall. A pale glow suffused the room, casting shadows everywhere.

That's when Timmy finally saw what he had fallen into. His breath caught in his throat and he wanted to scream, but he was far too terrified for his voice to work.

Lying on either side of him, peering through the clear plastic, was the dull, lifeless eyes of two dead children. On the closest body, the tongue protruded from the small mouth, now black and swollen. Maggots could be seen crawling on the face. He looked away, but only ended up staring at the other dead face lying on the other side of him. He was like the meat in between two pieces of bread.

Timmy couldn't scream; he was paralyzed with fear!

Charlie and Susan walked down the few remaining steps and stood over the boy.

"Well, young man, it looks like you found the other children who didn't want to play with us. Are you sure you don't want to change your mind now?" Charlie asked.

Timmy just stared at the dead faces of the two children. Then he started to cry, the tears blurring his vision. He barely noticed when Charlie picked him up and carried him back upstairs.

Susan followed, and when she was once more at the top of the stairs, she looked back down at the two small corpses lying on the cellar floor. Then she flicked the light off, casting the cellar into darkness once more; the door closing with a soft click; the small cadavers alone once more with noting but the maggots to keep them company.

Chapter Thirteen

*T*HE CAB SLOWED just after crossing the George Washington Bridge. Rupert leaned closer to the driver's face and could see the man was trying to think very hard. He kept scratching his head, as if he was wondering how the hell he had managed to leave the city without remembering it. Rupert took that as his cue to leave. At the next intersection, when the cab slowed down for a red light, Rupert slid out the window. The light turned green and the cab pulled away. Rupert quickly ran to the sidewalk to get out of the traffic that was even now buzzing by him.

He stood on the corner, not knowing where to go when he saw a gnome on a nearby lawn. This gnome was different from the one on Susan's lawn. This one had a longer beard and was missing a few layers of paint on a few places on his small body.

Rupert took a chance and walked over to the little guy. At first the gnome acted like Rupert wasn't there. He just faced forward, while holding a small pipe in his mouth. But then Rupert saw his eyes move. They swiveled left and right in their sockets, the gnome making sure the coast was clear. Most people were already freaked out by the small yard gnomes and had no idea why, but on a subconscious level, most human beings could sense that a yard gnome was more than it looked.

The gnome looked up at Rupert and grinned.

"Are you the guy looking for the kid?" It asked curtly.

Rupert nodded and leaned down closer to the yard gnome, and by doing that the smaller creature didn't have to tip its head up and risk discovery.

"Yes, that's me; do you know where he is?" He asked, hopefully.

The gnome gestured with his pipe to the left. "Pretty much, just follow that street for a couple of miles and when it comes to a T, go right. Once you get to that point you should be close enough to sense him." The gnome's eyes grew to slits and it leaned over to get closer to Rupert's face. "You do have his scent, don't you?"

Rupert stood up, insulted. "Of course I do, but even I couldn't track the boy from another city or across the bridge I just went over. Once I'm closer to him, I can take it from there."

The gnome nodded. "Fair enough." He looked up into Rupert's face and frowned. "Well, what are you waiting for, dummy? Get moving."

Rupert waved to the rude, little gnome and moved on, but the gnome was nothing more than an inanimate statue again. A pair of joggers had appeared at the end of the street and would soon be running by, so the gnome had returned to character before he was spotted.

Rupert walked down the sidewalk, looking at all the houses, with their flowers on their walkways and the well groomed lawns. For a human, this must be a nice place to live, he thought. But he still missed his apartment underground.

There was something about the security of being hundreds of feet under the earth that humans could never understand.

With the sun high in the sky, he walked down the street, still enjoying the day and looking forward to being reunited with Timmy once more.

*　　*　　*

Timmy had no idea where he was, his mind on autopilot. He kept seeing flashes of the dead children's eyes and he retreated further into his mind.

Charlie carried him back to the kitchen and sat him in a kitchen chair.

This was where before, Susan had slipped him some kind of sleep drug in his orange juice, but this time Charlie just opened his mouth and dropped a couple of drops of the drug on his tongue by using an eye dropper.

Timmy made a face at the sour tasting medicine, but managed to swallow it. Charlie took a step back and both adults looked down at him, waiting for something to happen. They talked for a few minutes, sometimes arguing it seemed, until Timmy's eyes started to feel heavy again. He tried to keep them open, but they refused, and soon he was unconscious once again.

Before he could fall off the chair, Charlie picked him up and carried him back to his new bedroom with the Spiderman sheets.

Dropping the boy onto the bed, he covered him up and then walked back to the door. Susan was waiting for him and she looked over his shoulder at the sleeping Timmy.

"What if he doesn't give in, like the others?" She asked in a neutral voice that held no emotion.

Charlie pushed by her and closed the door, this time locking it.

"Not a problem, hon'. It's just as easy to dig three graves as it is for two."

Then he walked away, back to the playroom. Mark and Janice were waiting and while they were well trained, the spirit taken out of them, he still didn't like leaving them unattended for too long at a time.

Hours later, Timmy woke slowly.

His head hurt and his mouth was bone dry once again. He sat up in the bed, the sheets falling into his lap. Through bleary eyes he looked around again and realized he was back where he had started.

Slipping off the bed, he went to the door and tried to open it. The door was locked. Letting the doorknob go, he turned around and looked at the room for the second time that day. His heart felt heavy and a feeling of dread suffused him. He leaned against the door and slid to the floor. Putting his head in his hands, he started to cry again. He was so scared and he wanted his mom, but he knew no matter how hard he wished it, that wasn't going to happen.

He sat there crying for almost an hour when he heard footsteps outside in the hallway. A pressure on the door caused him to roll away and look up at the face of Susan. She smiled down at him, the happy face now returned to her countenance, but Timmy had seen the real Susan and knew it was all for show.

She knelt down next to him and he cringed away from her.

"Now come on, honey, you need to cooperate with me. Why don't you come back into the playroom and we'll see what develops, hmm?"

Timmy shook his head. "No, leave me alone! I want my mom!" He screamed, trying to get as far from her as he could.

She grimaced and stood up, the smile long gone. "Fine, kid, be that way. You're only hurting yourself. If you don't want to play with me and Charlie then there really is no reason to keep you here." She moved back to the half-open door and stepped halfway out. "You just think about that for a while and if I were you, I'd have a different answer for me when I come back." Then she closed the door, the lock clicking in the quiet room, the small sound like a cannon shot to Timmy's ears in its finality.

Timmy started to cry again.

He stood up and went over to the one window in the room, looking outside at the normal looking street. Wishing he was on the other side of the metal bars like a prisoner sentenced to life in jail, he sighed. The metal bars were a stark contrast to the rest of the house's architecture, but they weren't there for beauty, but to keep him and the other children locked up inside.

He leaned against the window, the glass warm from the sun, and sighed again, the sniffles still coming, but the crying slowing for a few moments.

He was ready to just give up and do what they wanted of him, despite the fact he knew it was both gross and wrong. But thinking of the dead children in the basement reminded him of what would happen to him if he didn't cooperate.

He was just about to step away from the window and go cry on the bed some more when he almost jumped out of his skin at the sight of a dark shadow blocking the window.

On the opposite side of the glass stood Rupert. He had appeared from around the side of the house and his mouth curved up into a smile, fangs showing on both sides of his mouth.

"Hi, Timmy, I found you. I've been looking for you ever since you ran away from me at the bus station. What are you doing in that house?"

"Oh my God, Rupert?" He blinked in surprise and then realized there was hope where none existed moments before. "Rupert, there's some bad people in here and they want me to do things I don't want to do. You've got to get me out of here!" Timmy pleaded.

Rupert looked left and right and then back through the glass. "But how? I can't touch anything enough to get you out of there. You'll have to do it on your own."

Timmy looked confused. "But when you were at my house we played games and stuff. You could touch things then, why not now?"

Rupert sighed. "It's complicated, Timmy, but it has to do with you and your aura. Plus, that was my designated assignment, under your bed, I mean. There was residual energy left from the portal that let me touch things in your room, but out here there's nothing, no energy for me to tap into. You need to figure out how to get out of there on your own. I'm sorry."

Timmy started to cry again, the tears flowing down his cheeks. "But how? I don't know what to do and I'm scared. I wish I never left home."

Rupert felt so helpless, but there was nothing he could do. The sun reflected off the window, the warm rays heating his fur.

That's when an idea struck him.

Waving in front of the window to get Timmy's attention, he moved as close to the glass as he could get.

"Wait, Timmy, I think I might have thought of a way for you to get out of there, but you might need to find a few things first."

Timmy slowed his crying and nodded. "Okay, what do I do?"

Rupert grinned and then started to tell Timmy his idea. He didn't know if it would work, but their options were severely limited, and at the moment this seemed to be Timmy's only hope.

With Timmy nodding and asking questions when he wasn't sure about something in the plan, Rupert explained his idea. Timmy listened carefully, expecting the bedroom door to open at any moment, and Susan or Charlie to be there ready to take him back to the playroom.

When Rupert was finished, Timmy nodded and stepped away from the window. Now all he could do was wait for the adults to come get him and see if Rupert's idea would work or just end up getting him hurt… or worse, have him end up in the basement with the other dead children.

Chapter Fourteen

Twenty minutes after Rupert finished telling his plan to Timmy, the boy heard footsteps coming from the hall. Seconds later, the door creaked open and Susan stood framed in the doorway.

"Well, what have you decided?" She asked nicely.

Timmy stood up from his place on the floor, his back leaning against the bed.

"I'll come with you, I'll be good," he said in a downcast voice, his eyes looking down at his feet.

Susan frowned slightly. "Oh, don't be like that, Timmy. I promise, it'll be fun," she said, holding out her hand for him to take.

With a quick glance out the window to Rupert, who nodded encouragingly, Timmy took her hand and walked with her out into the hall and down to the playroom. Susan opened the door and the two of them stepped inside the brightly lit room. Charlie was at the tripod again, filming both Mark and Janice. The two children were in their underwear, and when Timmy walked in, Charlie looked up and grinned.

"Ah, excellent. So he agreed to cooperate?" He asked, looking at Susan.

She nodded. "Yes, he did. He finally saw reason."

"Good. Have him strip down to his underwear and then join the other two on the floor." Then he looked away from them and placed his eye against the view finder for the camera.

Timmy did as he was told, his legs shaking. He knew what these two adults were doing was wrong, but he didn't quite understand why. With his shirt off, he looked at both Mark and Janice. They watched him undress, their eyes both glassy and vacant.

With his shirt now off, Timmy started to undo his belt buckle, but then he stopped and turned around to look at Susan.

"Susan?" He asked her.

She sighed in frustration. "What is it now? What could you possibly want?"

Timmy made a sad face. "I'm sorry, but I have to go to the bathroom and I'm really thirsty. Could you take me? I promise I'll be quick."

"Can't you wait until later?" She asked, exasperated.

Timmy put his legs just a little closer together and shook his head no. "No, I really have to go. I'll be fast, I promise." He put on his best puppy dog face. The face that would always have his mother giving in to him.

Susan threw her hands in the air and swore under her breath. "Fine, let's go. And you better be quick."

Timmy smiled and nodded and then ran to the door. She opened it, and with Timmy in the lead, they moved down the hall. At the bathroom door, she opened it and waved him in.

"Hurry up, I want to get back there and finish the damn movie," she told him.

Nodding, he slipped into the bathroom, his body rubbing hers when she wouldn't move. When he was fully inside, he stopped and turned to look at her.

"Can I close the door a little?"

"Fine, whatever, just hurry the hell up." Then she proceeded to mumble under her breath. But then her cell phone rang. Distracted by the call, she answered it, Timmy forgotten while she talked.

Timmy closed the door and ran to the toilet. He reached up for the book of matches on the wall-shelf and brought them to him, holding them like they were gold. Taking the roll of toilet paper off the wall-clip, he ran over to the small closet in the corner of the bathroom, opened it, and placed the toilet paper inside. Rupert had told him to collect as much paper as he could find, so he grabbed all the magazines that were on the floor in a small magazine rack near the toilet.

As fast as he could, he crumpled them up and tossed them onto the top shelf of the closet. He had to stand on his tip-toes to reach, but he managed easily. Once the magazines were ripped up, he uncoiled the toilet paper roll, and after gathering it into a ball, threw the big fluffy ball on top of the magazines.

Susan was still talking on her cell phone, but Timmy knew he only had seconds before she checked on him, so he lit the first match in the matchbook and then carefully brought the tiny flame to the pile of paper.

One strip of toilet paper had slipped off the shelf and Timmy lit it carefully.

Like a fuse connected to dynamite, the strip of toilet paper caught fire and immediately burst into flames. The flame followed up the strip until reaching the large pile of soft kindling.

In a whoosh of bright flames, the paper started to burn. Timmy closed the closet door and then ran to the bathroom door to leave. But before he opened it, he stopped and ran back to the toilet. Flushing the toilet, he then dashed back to the door and slipped out into the hallway.

He closed the bathroom door behind him and smiled up at Susan. She barely noticed him, too engrossed with her phone call. He tugged on her shirt and she looked down at him. Placing her hand on the back of his head, she pushed him in front of her and back down the hall to the playroom.

Timmy complied and was soon back in front of the camera, with Susan standing in the far end of the room, still on the phone.

Charlie turned to look at her and ran a hand across his neck, telling her to hang up the phone. She simply flipped him off and turned away from him.

Charlie gestured for him to take off his pants and Timmy did as he was told. Both Mark and Janice were naked now and Timmy saw they were doing things his parent's used to do. As Mark moved on top of her, Janice seemed to barely notice, her eyes looking up at the ceiling like she was seeing someplace else.

Charlie told him to move next to Janice and place his penis near her face. Shaking and disgusted with what he was being made to do, he moved closer. Just as he kneeled down on the floor near the dazed girl's face, a high-pitched beeping sounded from outside the room. Charlie looked up from the monitor screen, clearly upset by yet another interruption, and Susan stopped talking to perk her head up in curiosity.

Timmy stood perfectly still, his heart in his throat. He could only pray Rupert's plan would work so he could leave this terrible place.

Charlie walked over to the door leading back into the hallway, waving to the three children. "You guys can take a break while I see what's going on," he said angrily.

Susan ignored him, still concentrating on her phone call.

Mark sat back on his butt, doing what he was told. Timmy saw his penis was standing straight up like his did when he woke up in the morning. It made him think of his step-dad when he would climb into his bed at night and he felt himself growing sick.

He looked away then, and stared at some of the toys on the wall, trying to think of other things. With Janice lying naked in front of him, her legs wide open, it only made it harder for him to accomplish this. He was fascinated with the way her groin looked so different from his.

For one thing, she had no penis. How in the world did she go to the bathroom?

He was pulled from his reverie when Charlie started screaming from outside in the hallway.

"Holy shit, Susan! The goddamn house is on fire!" He yelled excitedly while running back into the playroom. Susan hung up her phone then and turned to look at Charlie, but from the smoke pouring into the room from behind him, she didn't need him to repeat what he had just screamed.

"What, but how! Oh my God, what the hell are we going to do?" Then she regained a little control and ran over to Charlie, the children ignored for the moment. "Well, don't just stand there, get the fucking fire extinguisher and put it out," she ordered him.

He looked at her and nodded, then dashed off to the kitchen. Ten seconds later, he returned with a fourteen inch, red, fire extinguisher in his hands.

"I got it," he gasped.

She looked at him like he was the biggest idiot on Earth.

"That's great, dear, but how about putting out the friggin' fire with it?"

He blinked twice and then seemed to realize what she had just said.

"What? Oh, of course. Stay here, I'll be right back."

"As if I'd follow you. Dumb ass," she muttered to his back as he charged back to the bathroom.

Smoke began to fill the room, causing Timmy and the other two children to start coughing. So far neither adult had figured out that Timmy had started the fire.

With Susan occupied, Timmy slowly started to get dressed again. He reached for Mark and Janice's clothes and shoved them into their arms, motioning for them to get dressed. They copied him and in less than a minute were dressed also.

Charlie ran back into the playroom, coughing uncontrollably. "The damn fire's too big; half the bathroom is on fire and it looks like it got into the ceiling. We're fucked. We need to get out of here, now!"

"What! Are you serious? And what exactly are we supposed to do with all of this?" She said, waving her hands around the room. "Should we just leave it for the fire department to find? Not to mention what's in the basement?"

Charlie's eyes lit up with fear. "Oh, no, what the hell are we going to do? We are so screwed."

Everyone turned their heads to the front wall of the house when sirens could be heard coming from the street.

"Shit, the goddamn fire department! Someone must have called them," Susan spat.

Timmy was standing now and was looming over both Mark and Janice. He tried to pick them up, but they resisted. Whatever they had been given gave them almost no will of their own. Timmy wanted to help them, but realized he would have to worry about himself and hopefully he could tell someone about the two children when he escaped.

He watched Charlie and Susan arguing about what they should do, while the smoke grew thicker in the house. All the windows were closed, the smoke having nowhere to go, and the oxygen was quickly becoming scarce.

Timmy decided it was now or never, and with his shirt over his mouth and staying low like they had taught him in school, he ran out the playroom door.

Running as fast as he could, and coughing more with every breath, he made it to the front door of the house. Banging on the door repeatedly, he felt himself becoming dizzy from lack of oxygen. Then he heard voices on the other side of the door.

"Hello, is anyone in there? If you can hear me, we're coming in," a voice called from the other side of the door.

With the last of his strength, Timmy moved away from the door and fell to the carpet. He barely heard the sound of banging as the door was knocked in by a man in a bright yellow jacket. He wore a mask over his face and a big ax was in his left hand. He immediately saw Timmy and scooped him up in his arms.

"I got one," he said into the two-way radio in his mask.

Timmy pointed deeper into the house with his finger.

"Two more kids… adults mean…made us do bad stuff." Then he passed out from inhaling too much smoke.

The masked fireman looked down at Timmy, not understanding what he meant, then another fireman came through the door.

"The kid said there are more people in the house, including more kids. Get moving."

The second fireman nodded, the gesture barely seen with his mask on. Then both he and another fireman went into the house. Windows were being shattered by axes to let air into the burning home, the metal bars ripped from their moorings, and a large fire-hose was pushed into the burning house through one of the windows.

Timmy found himself being carried out of the house and onto the sidewalk, then he was gently laid on the soft grass of the front lawn. He blinked up at the sun as an oxygen mask was placed over his face by a paramedic.

Rupert was there, looking down on him.

Timmy blinked up at him, the oxygen making him feel better.

"Hi, Rupert, it worked, just like you said. Did I do good?"

Rupert smiled. "You sure did, great job, Timmy."

One paramedic looked to another one and then down at Timmy.

"Who the hells Rupert? What's this kid talking about?"

The second paramedic shrugged. "Who knows? Probably just disoriented from smoke inhalation. He should be fine in a little while."

Timmy looked up at the paramedic and blinked; then he tried to sit up.

"Whoa there, sport, take it easy. Just relax and lie down, you breathed in a lot of smoke," the first paramedic told him.

Timmy ignored him and pulled the mask from his face. "No, you don't understand. I was locked in there. Charlie and Susan made me do stuff with two other kids. They wanted me to kiss and stuff and Mark put his thing in Janice. It was gross. That's why I set the fire so you would come and rescue us."

Paramedic One looked at Paramedic Two.

"Did you hear what he just said, Dick?"

"Yeah, but it can't be true. That's crazy, but then you never know."

He stood up then and waved over a police officer. Timmy lay back down, watching the paramedic tell the officer what he had just said.

The police officer frowned and then spoke into the two-way radio on his chest.

Seconds later, more policemen came over. Timmy saw firemen carrying Mark and Janice out of the house now, both being laid down on the grass near him.

Then Charlie and Susan were helped out. Both were coughing heavily and their clothes were covered in soot. A fireman escorted them to the back of an ambulance where they were given oxygen masks.

Both took them greedily, sucking in the fresh air. Three policemen went over to them and started asking both of them questions. At first everything seemed casual, almost routine, until two firemen walked out of the house with the two dead children from the basement. The plastic bags were both wet and singed from the fire and the water used to put it out. The two small bodies were gently placed on the lawn and then a fireman waved one of the police officers over to him.

Timmy sat up now, watching everything. Rupert was by his side and he could feel the warm fur against his cheek.

The fireman and the police officer talked for a few seconds, the officer looking down at the two bodies. Then he spoke into his radio again.

Timmy looked over at Charlie and Susan to see them both violently thrown to the grass. The two officers sat on top of them and handcuffed them both. Then they were pulled to their feet and carried away.

Through a swarm of moving bodies, Timmy saw both adults placed into the back of a squad car. From the look on their faces, they didn't look happy about it.

Timmy smiled at Rupert. "We did it. Those bad people are going to leave me alone, but what do I do now? When the policemen find out who I am they'll call my step-dad."

"Then we need to get out of here. The moment no ones looking we can sneak away. Then we can get back to the city. But are you sure you don't just want to go home now, Timmy?" Rupert asked.

Timmy shook his head. "Yeah, I want to go home, but not before I see my grandpa. It's the only way my step-dad will leave me alone. I have no choice."

"Okay, Timmy, but I had to ask," Rupert said.

Timmy sat quiet then, with chaos swarming around him, waiting for the right time to slip away. It didn't take long for a determined Timmy to move away unnoticed and soon he was a few blocks away; just another kid walking around on the suburban streets.

Timmy stopped and looked over his shoulder at the houses behind him. A column of smoke drifted over the nearby homes and was disbursed by the wind.

Rupert was next to him, and as the two moved further away from the fire, Timmy looked up at his big, furry face.

"So how do we get back to the bus station so I can get to my grandpa's house?" Timmy asked innocently.

Rupert frowned. "Timmy, I have no idea, but give me a chance, will ya. I mean, I did just get you out of that house."

"Yeah, I guess, but I had to set the place on fire. My mom told me to never play with matches. If she finds out what I did, I'll be punished for the rest of my life."

"I think she'll let you off the hook on that one, Timmy. From what you've told me, I think it would be considered special circumstances."

"Special circum…special circums… What's that mean?" Timmy asked, giving up on trying to pronounce the word.

Rupert chuckled. "It means that it was probably okay that you set the house on fire, but you shouldn't do it again. Promise, okay?"

Timmy nodded, "Okay, I promise, no more fires."

Then hand in hand, the two unlikely friends continued down the sidewalk, the sounds of the emergency sirens slowly fading away.

CHAPTER FIFTEEN

TIMMY'S FEET HURT him something awful.

He couldn't remember the last time he had walked so much. Both he and Rupert had been walking for more than an hour and he really wanted to rest.

A soda can was in his way on the sidewalk and he kicked it halfheartedly out of his path.

"Rupert, when are we gonna get a ride back to the bus station? I'm hungry and my feet hurt."

Rupert shrugged his large, purple shoulders. "I'm really sorry about that, Timmy, but I'm all out of ideas."

Timmy pouted. He had lost his backpack back at Susan's house. Now all he had was a few dollars and miscellaneous change in his pocket. The surrounding buildings were all domestic, not even one 7-11 or grocery store in sight. For the hundredth time since he had left his house, he wished he could just call his mom and go home. But he knew that would be a big mistake, even worse than running away. He had to get to his grandpa's house, only then would he truly be safe.

Timmy slowed as they came to a four way intersection. A large two-way bridge could be seen peeking over some of the distant houses and further off on the horizon were some of the grander skyscrapers of New York City, blending together and looking like tall, skinny caricatures of mountains.

"I still don't see why you can't carry me," Timmy stated as they walked.

"I told you before, Timmy, no one else can see me. It's part of the connection we share when I was assigned to you, so if I did pick you up, anyone watching would see a small boy floating in the air. Do you have any idea the kind of trouble I'd get into if my supervisor found out about that?" He shook his head. "No way am I getting into that kind of trouble. Besides, if my supervisor finds out I'm helping you run around your world, I'll probably get demoted, or worse, fired. On my world, if you're not scaring, you're nothing."

"I'm sorry, Rupert, it's just that I'm tired, that's all."

Timmy plopped down onto the curb, his feet landing in the gutter. He placed his head in his hands and let out a groan.

"I'm so hungry," he moaned. Then he looked up at Rupert. "Are you hungry, Rupert? Since I met you, I haven't seen you eat anything."

Rupert scratched his head and grinned. "I can't eat anything from your world, Timmy. I can only eat in mine. That's why I go back to my world every morning."

"But you haven't gone back yet. Are you gonna get in trouble?"

Rupert scratched his head and thought about that one.

He watched a few cars go by and then looked down at Timmy.

"You know, I really haven't given it much thought. There's a lot of bureaucracy where I'm from and it's really possible no one even knows I'm gone."

"Bureaucracy? What's that?" He asked, sounding the word out.

Rupert bit his lower lip, thinking how to explain bureaucracy to an eight-year-old boy.

"Let's just say that there are so many people doing so many things on my world that it takes a while for one person to find out what another person is doing. From what I hear, it's a lot like your government."

Timmy looked up at his friend's face. "I wouldn't know, I'm only eight."

Rupert stood over him, not knowing what to say to that. He watched the different vehicles drive by, some stopping at the traffic light and then continuing on when the light would turn green. It amused him and reminded him of Monster City. He wondered if the humans knew about his world, how surprised they would be to see just how much his fellow monsters had in common with humans.

He was pulled away from his daydreaming when Timmy moaned again.

"Rupert, I'm so hungry," he said again.

Rupert looked up when an open-bed pickup truck pulled up to the traffic light. The truck was the third vehicle in line, and at the moment no other cars were on the street. Rupert immediately had an idea and bent down to look at Timmy. Timmy sensed more than felt the movement and looked up.

Rupert pointed to the truck. "Timmy, right now before the light changes, go run and get into the back of that pickup truck."

"Why?" Timmy asked, curious.

"Because it's a free ride back into the city, now hurry up before the light changes."

Timmy saw the pickup and understanding flashed in his head. "Great idea, Rupert. We'll hitchhike."

"Exactly," Rupert said.

The first car at the intersection started to move when the light changed back to green.

The pickup started moving as well and would soon be moving too fast to catch.

Timmy and Rupert were no more than ten feet from the back of the truck and Timmy ran as fast as he could. With Rupert's help, he jumped into the bed and hid under an old tarp under the rear window. The driver heard and felt the slight shift on the vehicle's shocks when Timmy's sleight weight climbed into the back, but a quick glance in his rearview mirror showed nothing amiss, so he went back to singing with a country song playing on the truck's radio. With nothing but open road in front him, the driver stepped on the gas pedal, the vehicle surging forward.

Rupert was slightly behind Timmy, but the pickup pulled away before Rupert could catch up.

Timmy eyes opened wide as he realized his friend wasn't going to make it. "Rupert, hurry up!" He called, the driver hearing nothing as he wailed to Waylon Jennings in the driver's seat.

Rupert ran after the receding pickup truck, his muscles pumping under his purple fur. It only took a few seconds for him to realize he wouldn't make it.

"Its okay, Timmy, I'll get back some other way. You stay there and make it back to the bus station. Wait for me where that bus driver found you in the luggage compartment. I'll catch up to you as soon as I can!" He called slowing down, breathing heavily.

Timmy nodded, and with tears in his eyes, reached his right hand out, as if he could pull Rupert to him with just the power of his thoughts. The truck picked up speed and soon Rupert was lost from sight. Timmy dropped his hand and sighed. He wasn't scared, at least not yet. He found he was becoming less and less frightened each time something went wrong. He had no idea he was simply adapting to life on the run, or better yet, life on the streets.

Timmy was alone again, and though he knew his friend would catch up to him eventually, he still wished he was with him.

While the cool wind dried the tears on his face, the pickup's driver slowed at the toll booth, paid the bridge toll, and then headed over the massive structure of steel and cement.

Timmy was on his way back to New York, and hopefully, his monster under his bed wouldn't be too far behind.

Chapter Sixteen

*R*UPERT SLOWED HIS frantic pace, realizing he couldn't run fast enough to catch the speeding pickup truck. His pumping legs slowed and he moved to the side of the street, not wanting to tempt fate by having an automobile drive through his body.

His heart was heavy as the pickup disappeared around a bend in the road. He had just found Timmy and had lost him again in the blink of an eye.

All in all, he wasn't much of a chaperone for the boy.

Now he had to figure out how to get back into the city again quickly before something happened to his young charge yet again.

Walking in the gutter, he hadn't covered more than a hundred feet when he slowed his progress. He stopped in front of a two-family house with white clapboard and brown shutters. But that wasn't what had attracted Rupert's attention. He could have cared less about the house itself. What had caught his eyes was a lion statue sitting in the front yard.

From where he stood, he could sense the statue wasn't all it appeared to be, so he detoured from the street and crossed the bright-green lawn until he was no more than two feet away from the statue.

The statue did nothing but simply sat there.

After all, it was just a statue.

Rupert folded his arms and frowned.

"I know you're one of us," Rupert said. "I could smell you from the moment I looked over here."

The statue remained inanimate.

"Look, help me out and there's five bucks in it for you," Rupert cajoled.

The statue's eyes opened and looked directly at Rupert. "Ooh, big spender. Make it a twenty and you've got yourself a deal."

Rupert sighed. "Fine, but I'll have to owe you."

The statue looked him up and down as if he was sizing him up.

"Well, okay. But only because your kind usually keeps his word."

"Relax, you'll get your money. Besides, what could you possibly need money for anyway?"

The statue shrugged, a few pieces of plaster falling away from its shoulders from the gesture. "I'm a sucker for the ponies. So what do you want? I already saw you lose the kid. Maybe if you weren't so fat you could have caught him."

Rupert looked down at his waist and frowned. "Hey, I'm not fat, that's just winter weight."

The lion statue chuckled. "Winter weight? Sure, and I'm really a sphinx in disguise."

"Look, are you going to help me or not?"

The lion statue sighed. "Fine, what can I do for you?"

"I need you to tell the monster grapevine that Timmy is heading back to New York and that if anyone sees him to pass it on."

"So you're that fat, purple guy everyone is talking about, huh? And I suppose that was the boy? Wow, you lost him already huh, you're good, aren't you?"

Rupert said nothing, his eyes creasing in anger.

"Fine, I can do that, but I need one more thing from you."

"What, what is it?" Rupert asked impatiently.

The statues eyes rolled up and looked up to its forehead. "Would you get that bird shit off my forehead? It's driving me crazy."

Rupert did as he was asked, scraping the statue with one of his claws. When he was finished, the statue grinned.

"Thanks, pal; I can't tell you what a relief that is. Do you have any idea what its like to be shit on all day?"

"Uhm, no actually. Look, I need to go. I've got a long walk back over that bridge if I can't catch a ride, so I've got to get going. Thanks again."

"Sure, anytime, just don't forget my cash. If you have to, you can give it to Rocky, I'm into him for a couple of hundred anyway, just tell him the money goes against my debt, he'll understand."

Rupert waved as he walked away. He grinned when he saw a pigeon land on the lion statue's head as he walked away.

"Don't you do it, you flying rat, I'm warning you!" The statue threatened.

Rupert chuckled and headed off down the street, his eyes constantly looking for suitable transportation to get him back to the city

*   *   *

Timmy's eyes were wide with excitement as the pickup truck turned onto a street that led into the business district of New York. Timmy's head darted back and forth as he watched the thousands of people running and walking on the sidewalks. Men in three-piece suits and overcoats and women in power suits walked with purpose, more than half with cell phones glued to their ears.

Timmy was amazed.

This was nothing like his hometown in Virginia. The pickup slowed at the entrance to a parking garage and Timmy figured it would be as good a time as any to jump ship. When the truck stopped to take a parking ticket, Timmy climbed out from under the tarp and dropped to the street.

A man driving a blue Volvo was waiting behind the pickup truck to enter the parking garage and his eyebrows went up in surprise as he watched a small boy climb out from the bed of the truck and slip away into the crowd of pedestrians.

The boy was gone before the man could have done anything even if he'd wanted to, so with a shrug, he forgot about it and followed the truck into the parking garage.

Timmy had to stay against the buildings or risk being caught in an avalanche of bodies and legs. No one paid him the slightest bit of attention, each person having their own agendas. He walked by a pay phone and a pang of homesickness coursed through him. A tiny voice in his head screamed to him to just use the phone and call home. Better yet, maybe he should call his grandpa. His grandpa could drive to New York from Boston and save him. That would be a great idea. Timmy decided he would do just that and worked his way through the mass of pedestrians until he was at the payphone.

Reaching into his pocket, he pulled out a quarter. Dropping it into the phone, he prepared to call his grandpa, his finger hovering over the buttons, when he realized he had no idea what the phone number was or what the actual address to their house was. He thought back to his house and the small, brown address book that contained all the names and numbers of family members and friends that sat near the phone in the living room.

Realizing he wouldn't be calling his grandpa anytime soon, he hung up the phone and left the phone booth.

Timmy kept moving, not really knowing where he was going. People huddled against the buildings, wearing nothing more than rags and smelling like they hadn't bathed in years. Every one of them held cups or hats in their hands and Timmy watched as people walking by would give them spare change, and sometimes even dollars.

Timmy felt his stomach grumbling again, reminding him he hadn't eaten in quite a while.

With his head low, he continued walking, he had no idea where the bus station was and he was afraid to ask anyone. After all, the last time someone had tried to help him, he ended up being kidnapped!

With his stomach rumbling and a few tears preparing to fall from his eyes yet again, he walked deeper into the city, wondering exactly just how he was supposed to find his way back to the bus station in a city he had never been in before.

Chapter Seventeen

*T*IMMY TURNED THE corner at the next intersection and paused in mid-stride. There was a small grocery store halfway down the street and sitting on a table in front of the store were boxes filled with produce and fruit. His stomach growled for the hundredth time and Timmy swallowed what saliva he had in his mouth.

He was so hungry it hurt.

He reached into his pocket and pulled out all the change he had. Counting slowly, he realized he had two dollars and twenty-eight cents. He frantically looked for the dollar bills he thought he still had, but soon came to the conclusion he must have lost them.

He had been saving the money for an emergency and had decided if he didn't eat soon he could starve. And now he was only down to his loose change. Grasping the change tightly, he breathed a sigh of relief. At least he had enough for a few pieces of fruit or maybe even a candy bar.

He shook his head, wondering how he could possibly starve in a big city, surrounded by thousands of people. With the money in his hand, he started walking toward the grocery store, his mouth already watering as he thought about biting into a juicy apple or maybe a banana.

When he was less than a dozen feet from the front of the store, a man on a bicycle crashed into him. Timmy tried to get out of his way, but the man was moving to fast. Timmy only had time to see the backpack and the radio clipped to the man's shirt before both he and the cyclist crashed into each other.

The cyclist went head first over his bicycle, landing in a pile of trash set out for trash pick-up. Timmy was knocked to the sidewalk and his hands opened instinctively to catch himself from hitting his head on the concrete.

The loose change in his hands fell from his opened palm to roll and bounce away across the sidewalk.

Before he had realized what had happened, three different homeless people had swarmed out onto the sidewalk and quickly scooped up the loose change.

Pedestrians yelled and cursed at the bums as they got in their way, but otherwise, the bums were left alone. Before Timmy could so much as shout that the coins were his, the bums had collected all of it and had then disappeared down the street.

Timmy climbed to his feet and started running after them, yelling that they had his money, but after less than a quarter of a block, he realized it was hopeless.

With his head hanging low, he walked back to the store, hoping he could find some of the coins the bums had possibly missed.

While avoiding the pedestrians on the crowded sidewalk, he managed to find only fifty cents of his lost funds. When he was sure he had found as much as he could, he walked over to the grocery store.

An Asian man with an apron stood in front of the store with a broom in his hand. Timmy walked up to him and smiled.

"Mister, I lost all my money. I only have fifty cents left. How much is an apple or maybe a banana?"

The man looked down at the small boy in front of him with no mercy in his eyes.

"An apple is seventy five cents and a banana is sixty or so. I don't know kid, it depends on the size."

Timmy looked at the two quarters in his hand and sighed. "I've only got fifty cents."

The man shrugged. "Then your shit out of luck, aren't you. Now get out of here before I call the cops. Shouldn't you be in school or something?"

Timmy took one step back from the man, not quite believing what he'd just heard.

How could this man be so mean to him?

Timmy took one more step away from the man and looked to his right. The boxes of fruit were next to him. All he had to do was just reach out and the fruit would be his.

"Go on, scram!" The man yelled.

Timmy's stomach rumbled yet again and despite the fact he was terrified, he did something he had never, ever, done in his short life…he stole something.

Reaching out with both hands, he grabbed an apple in each hand.

"Hey, you little bastard, put those down!" The store owner yelled.

Timmy heard him yell, and with apples in hand, turned and ran away as fast as he could.

"Hey, come back here! You've got to pay for those, dammit!" The owner called after him, actually running a few feet after Timmy.

Timmy ran quick, dodging in and out of the pedestrians until the grocery store was a few streets away.

The store owner decided it wasn't worth it and went back to his store, shaking the broom in his hands angrily.

When Timmy couldn't run anymore, he slowed and looked over his shoulder. No one was following him. His heart pounded in his chest and he had never been as scared as he was right now.

People flowed around him, no one giving him the slightest glance. If anyone was curious what an eight-year-old boy was doing in the middle of New York, then no one asked him.

Timmy started to walk again, his breathing coming in gasps. He looked at one of the apples and his stomach rumbled. Then he took his first bite, and as the sweet juices ran down his chin, he truly felt he had never tasted something as sweet as the apple in his hand.

He continued to eat while he walked and after many blocks were behind him, he slowed, now having to wait to cross a wide street.

People stood all around him with their briefcases and cell phones in their hands.

Timmy looked around him and his eyes went wide when he saw a sign on one of the lamp posts. It read: BUS STATION, 1 MILE.

The light changed and he went with the flow, crossing the street and then stopping on the other side. He looked up at the sign, at the arrow pointing further down the next street, and he smiled.

He had no idea how he could have possibly found the bus station again, but it looked like he had. Chewing on the second apple, his stomach feeling better with some food in it, he walked down the sidewalk. While he was still a long way from home, for the first time in what seemed like a long while, he felt pretty good about his situation. It looked like things were working out and would be fine. Now all he had to do was wait for Rupert and then he could get to his grandparent's house.

Once there, he could put this entire ordeal behind him.

* * *

Two black men stood on the street corner and watched Timmy walk by. The boy barely noticed them, lost in his own thoughts.

One man looked to the other and smiled.

"Hey, Clarence, isn't that the same white boy we saw at the bus station yesterday?"

Clarence watched the boy walk by and then nodded. "Shit, Slim, you're right." He looked around the street, but the boy seemed alone. "Looks like that white bitch is gone, too. What do you say we go reintroduce ourselves to the little cracker?"

Slim smiled, his stained yellow teeth showing through cracked lips.

"Shit, Clarence, that's a damn good idea."

The two men started off, making sure to keep Timmy in sight. The boy had slipped through their fingers the first time they'd met and fortune had given the two men a second chance.

This time they would be quick and would make sure no one interfered.

Chapter Eighteen

*T*IMMY COULD SEE the side of the bus terminal and his mouth turned up into a big smile.

He had finally made it back to the bus station!

Now all he had to do is wait for Rupert to arrive and then the two of them could leave New York and head to Boston.

When Timmy was less than half a block from the bus station, he felt a heavy hand on his shoulder. The hand held tight, forcing him to stop walking. He turned around and the two men he'd first met after leaving the terminal glared down at him.

"Let me go, leave me alone," Timmy said, trying to escape, but the hand holding him was strong and felt like a vice. Timmy winced when the hand squeezed harder.

"Now, just wait a second there, little cracker. We just want to help you," Slim said, holding the boy tight.

"Yeah, little man, we're your friends. So, just calm down and let us talk to you," Clarence said near his ear.

Timmy tried to pull away again, but realizing it was hopeless, he quieted down.

"What do you mean you want to help me?" Timmy asked.

Slim smiled and bent closer to Timmy. Timmy winced at the man's redolence, his nose scrunching up as he tried to turn his face away. The man smelled like old cigarettes and alcohol.

"Listen, little man, we know that bitch that took you from us before wasn't your mom. Hell, I know a runaway when I see one. So if you want, I got a job for you. If you accept, there's a place for you to sleep and plenty to eat." He smiled; his yellow teeth making him look more malevolent than friendly. "So what do you say?"

"But I'm waiting for my friend. We got separated and he said to meet him at the bus station. I need to be here when he gets back," Timmy explained.

Clarence looked at Slim and the man shrugged. "When's he coming to meet you?" Clarence asked.

Timmy shook his head and shrugged. "I don't know. I just have to wait for him."

Slim let go of Timmy, trying to gain his trust. "Okay, but why don't you help me and my boy here out until he gets here. I tell you what. I've got people on the streets that see everything. One of them will keep an eye out for your friend, and when he sees him, he'll tell me. So what does your friend look like?"

Timmy looked up at the two men, deciding if he should tell them. He figured what did he have to lose, so he started in on his description of his friend.

"My friends name is Rupert and he's a little taller than you," Timmy said with a smile.

Clarence nodded. "Okay, that's good, and what color is he? White or black."

"He's purple," Timmy stated as if it was the most normal color to be in the world.

"Say what? Little cracker's been smokin' some of your shit, Slim," Clarence joked

Slim looked down at Timmy and frowned. "Did you say purple, little man?"

"Uh-huh, he has purple fur and big claws, but he's really nice and when I ran away he came with me to keep me safe, but everything keeps going wrong," Timmy said, a few tears beginning to collect in the corners of his eyes.

Slim looked around them, studying the street.

So far no one had paid them any attention, but their luck could run out at any moment. He needed to get them off the street before a cop spotted them. Two black men, who obviously looked like they sold drugs, standing with a white boy on the sidewalk near the bus station was unusual enough even in New York to raise a cop's suspicions.

"Listen, little man, that's not a problem. I'll get the word out and when we see him, we'll let you know. Until then, what do you say you come work for me?" Slim asked nicely. "Tell you what, the first thing we'll do is get a couple of hamburgers. You hungry, my man?"

Timmy's stomach grumbled a little. The two apples had been small, and while they had tasted great, they had disappeared into his mouth far too fast. The temptation of food was too much for him and he nodded and smiled.

"That would be great, I'm still pretty hungry."

Clarence slapped Timmy on the back gently. "Well, all right then, little man. There's a diner just around the block, let's go. After you," Clarence said, gesturing with his hand.

Timmy nodded and started down the sidewalk, moving out of the path of busy pedestrians. With the two men behind him it was a little easier as people seemed to move out of his way instead of the other way around.

With Timmy walking in front of them, Clarence and Slim talked between themselves.

"Are you sure about this, Slim? The kid's pretty young," Clarence said.

Slim patted his friends shoulder. "Relax, man, the boy's fine. Besides, you're never too young to become a drug mule."

Slim flashed his friend his teeth and then caught up to Timmy, acting like he was the boy's best friend. Clarence shook his head, still not sure, but he always deferred to Slim. If Slim said it was okay, then that was good enough for him.

The two men and the small boy walked onward, and were soon lost in the crowds on the sidewalk.

*   *   *

When Timmy had first been stopped by Clarence and Slim, the boy had no way of knowing that from just a few feet away in a storm drain, he was being watched. While the two men convinced him to leave with them, two beady eyes and a set of sharp teeth sat below, watching from the metal storm grate.

As the boy and the two men walked away, Rocky watched them go until his angle caused him to lose sight of them.

He dropped back onto the sewer floor and thought about what he'd seen. The boy had made it back to the city, but Rupert was nowhere to be found.

With small short legs, Rocky ran off down the tunnel. He had to spread the word and find out where Rupert was. He'd seen the two black men around before and knew they were trouble. If Rupert didn't get back soon and save the boy from them, then it wouldn't matter, because it would already be too late.

*   *   *

David slowed when he approached the exit for Boston.

When he had first left his house, he'd been hell-bent on finding Timmy, but after long hours alone in the car, he soon realized there was no chance in Hell he would ever be able to find the boy in a giant metropolis like New York.

But he had tried and miraculously won.

He'd beaten the odds and picked up the boy's trail.

Remembering back to the night before, Timmy had said something about going to see his grandfather before he'd run away from home, so David felt his best chance of finding the boy would be to stake out the grandfather's home in the suburbs of Boston and let the boy come to him.

Billy Conrad, Timmy's grandfather, was a pain in the ass. He had constantly butted into David's affairs and so, finally becoming fed-up, David had cut off all ties with him and his wife.

Timmy hadn't been happy about it, but as far as David was concerned, that was too damn bad. When the time came he would listen to what an eight year old said, he would turn in his balls, because he wasn't much of a man any more.

A slight grin crossed his lips as he sped off down the highway. Sooner or later the boy would show up at his grandfather's house and when he did, David would be waiting.

Chapter Nineteen

RUPERT CONTINUED WALKING, his purple fur blowing in the light breeze. After finally making it over the large bridge, Rupert had started into the city. He had been unable to find suitable transporta-tion and had walked the entire distance. Now, as the sun began to set, he realized he had been separated from Timmy for far too many hours. He hoped the boy was all right, but the chances were slim.

He could only hope once he returned to the bus station, Rocky would be around. Perhaps the sewer monster had heard something since Rupert and Timmy had been separated again.

Hoping he was going in the right direction, he trudged on.

Placing one large foot in front of the other, he headed deeper into the city.

*　　*　　*

Timmy was led down the busy streets of the city until Slim slowed in front of one particular building. The first floor was occupied by a small news stand, the other ten floors dedicated to apartments. A door on the side of the newsstand opened into a large hallway filled with other doors, an elevator and a stairwell leading upwards.

Slim ignored the elevator and pointed Timmy toward the stairs.

"Our place is up there, little man. The elevator doesn't work we gotta climb," Slim stated.

Timmy just stared at him and then gazed around the hallway. Graffiti covered the walls with lurid designs, looking like modern cave paintings, and as he was led further into the stairwell, he smelled the distinct odor of urine and decay.

Trash covered the floor and collected at the bottom of the stairs. He made a face, disgusted by the scenery.

"Looks like the boy don't like the living arrangements, Slim," Clarence stated, noticing Timmy's discomfort.

Slim shrugged. "Don't care, he'll get used to it," he said, climbing up the stairs.

Timmy was behind Slim, but in front of Clarence, so even if he thought to run, it would have been useless.

The threesome climbed to the second floor and Slim stepped out into the new hallway. Timmy stopped behind him. The sounds of people could be heard coming from the other side of the doors lining the hall. One door had a baby crying, the shrill sound penetrating through the other noise. Other doors had loud music playing or people arguing. The floor was covered with yet more trash and some large green trash bags with holes in their sides, the contents spilling out.

Once again the walls were covered in graffiti, the bright orange and red paints resembling some odd form of modern art.

Clarence nudged Timmy gently. "That way, little cracker. You're almost home."

Timmy did as he was told, Slim next to him. At the far end of the hallway a cracked and peeling wooden door sat inconspicuously, blending in with the wall. Slim pulled out a set of keys, and after a moment fussing with the door lock, opened the door and ushered Timmy inside.

The room was dark and smelled almost worse than the hallway. Slim slipped inside ahead of him and Clarence turned on a wall switch, bathing the room in a pallid, yellow glow.

Timmy moved into the room slowly.

The sound of the front door closing made him jump. For better or worse he was stuck here.

Clarence plopped down on the ripped and filthy sofa and placed his feet on the plywood coffee table.

"Have a seat, little man, and we'll fill you in on what you'll be doing. Once we're done, we'll get something to eat. Okay?" Clarence asked.

Timmy nodded.

Slim had grabbed a couple of beers from the refrigerator in the kitchen and now joined Clarence on the sofa. Timmy sat on an old milk crate, the size just right for his small form.

After cracking open the beer and taking a large gulp that finished off half the can, Slim set it on the make-shift coffee table and looked over at Timmy.

"All right, little man, let me lay it down for you," he said smoothly.

He proceeded to explain to Timmy that the two men were drug dealers and how they needed someone Timmy's age to deliver the goods to their customers. That way if Timmy was to get caught, he would be a minor and the two men would remain untouched. They explained how Timmy would go out and deliver the packages he was given and then how he would return for more orders. He was to take any money he received and keep it until he returned back to the apartment. If he did everything he was told, he would be fine, but if he got the idea to run, then the two men would track him down and make him pay. And if that wasn't enough of a threat, they told the young boy they would find his family and make them pay, too.

Timmy listened to the entire speech, his heart beating faster after every sentence. He quickly realized he was in trouble again. Not the kind of trouble as with Susan and Charlie, but a different kind, in some ways even more deadly. The two men sitting in front of him were bad men and would kill him if he didn't do what he said. Thinking about his mom and what these two would do to her made him realize he had to do whatever they said.

He was too young to realize they were just a couple of lowlife drug dealers who would never be able to find him again if he just ran away after his first delivery.

They had done an excellent job of intimidating the small child, and when Slim was done talking, the man looked Timmy square in the face.

"So, do you understand what I'm laying down to you? Do you get how serious our shit is?"

Timmy nodded. "Umm, yes, sir, I understand. Just don't hurt my mom."

Slim looked at Clarence and the two men chuckled. "Good, that's real good."

He stood up and threw the empty beer can he was holding into the corner of the room. It fell onto a pile of other refuse, and after rolling twice, lay still.

"Well, come on, man, I told you I'd get you a burger. There's a Mickey D's down the corner, is that cool?"

Timmy's eyes lit up. "McDonalds? Yeah, that would be great! Can I get a shake, too."

Opening the front door and stepping into the hallway, Slim smiled. "Sure, little man, a shake's cool with me."

The two men and their new employee walked down the stairwell and back into the sunlight. With Timmy looking forward to the restaurant, he now talked continually, the two men barely listening.

In moments they were swallowed up by the crowds of pedestrians and lost from sight.

* * *

A black Crown Victoria with tinted windows sat silently across the street from Clarence and Slims' apartment building, blending in with dozens of other cars parked bumper to bumper along the sidewalk.

The passenger had just reached for the door handle, prepared to step out, when the driver stopped him.

"Wait a second, Joey, where do you think you're going?" Sergeant Edward Hicks of the New York City Police Department's Narcotics Division asked.

Joey Falzone was a beat cop, just promoted to Narcotics Division and was eager to prove himself.

"I'm going after the two perps. We don't want to lose them."

Hicks leaned back in his seat and lit his third cigarette in an hour. He was trying to quit, but the damned things kept calling to him, and being on a boring stakeout only made it worse. What else was there to do but smoke and drink coffee?

"You're not going anywhere. Just sit back down and relax. Those two idiots will be back in an hour or so."

"What makes you so sure, Sergeant?"

"What makes me so sure is that I've been watching those two morons for a little over a week and I know their habits. They're probably going to get something to eat, or better yet, going to get more beer at the corner packy store. So just sit back and relax. Here," he said offering the young man a cigarette, "have one of these."

"No thanks, Sergeant, I don't smoke, and neither should you. Those things will kill you."

Hicks starting laughing, but stopped when it turned into a light coughing fit. "Kill me? Shit, Joey, I'm a cop. If I end up dying from lung cancer it'll be a goddamn miracle."

Joey sat silent, watching the pedestrians as they walked by for a while, lost in his private thoughts. A particularly pretty red-head went by his window and he found himself leaning forward to check her butt out in the passenger door's mirror. The small black words on the mirrored glass read: objects may appear larger than they appear. As he looked at the red-head's ass in the mirror, he didn't think that would be such a bad thing.

He was pulled from his reverie when Hicks sat up in his seat. "Hey, Joey, look who just got back," he said, gesturing out the window and across the street.

Joey looked where he was pointing and saw Clarence, Slim and the young boy returning from wherever they had gone.

As they moved closer, Joey could see the kid carrying a small toy from a happy meal and the two men each had a six pack of beer in their hands.

"See, what did I tell ya, those two idiots never leave their place for too long."

"How'd you know that?" Joey asked.

Hicks shrugged. "Simple, they've got all their stash in the apartment and they know they'd get jacked if they were gone for too long."

"So what's next? Are we just gonna watch them all day?" Joey inquired as he turned in his seat to admire another pretty lady while she walked down the sidewalk. Ever since Joey had seen Saturday Night Fever when he was younger he had always thought of himself to be like Tony, only handsomer.

Hicks blew smoke out the window and followed it with the rest of the cigarette, the butt rolling in the street to join a hundred others. Starting the car, he shifted the transmission into drive, then turned to look at Joey.

"No, we're done with that. They've got a kid with them now and that's where I draw the line." He pulled out into the street, a cab honking furiously. Flipping the cab off, he headed down the street, his destination the police precinct.

"What's the kid got to do with anything?" Joey asked.

Hicks slowed down at an intersection, the light red. He turned to stare at Joey and his face grew hard. "If those two idiots have a kid then that means only one thing. That they're about to start moving their product and I'm not gonna let that happen. Once we get back to the barn, I'm gonna get us a warrant for their arrests and then we are going to take those two bastards down…tonight."

Joey nodded, glad to finally be doing something other than sitting in a car all day. "That's friggin' great, but what about the kid?" Joey inquired.

"The kid will be fine; we'll just wait until the kid should be in bed and then we'll take 'em. But be aware, Joey, those two idiots aren't as stupid as they look. I happen to know they are very well armed and that's why we need to take them fast." The light changed and he stepped on the gas. "You up for this?" He asked, glancing askance to Joey.

"Shit, this is what I've been waiting for ever since I came to Narcotics Division."

"Good man," Hicks said and then concentrated on jockeying for position down the busy metropolitan street.

Once he had his warrant and night had fallen, he would be returning. Clarence and Slim were going to be receiving some unexpected company tonight.

Chapter Twenty

*R*UPERT SLOWED AS he approached the bus station. He had made many wrong turns before finally arriving at his destination. He had almost given up hope of ever finding the bus terminal until he had spotted a bus similar to the one Timmy and him had previously ridden on.

When the bus had slowed with the traffic, Rupert had jumped onto its rear bumper, his claws holding him in place. No one could see him, so it was child's play to ride the bus back to the bus terminal where he hoped, despite the long time it had taken him to return, that Timmy would still be there waiting for him. But then he had jumped off the bus after getting a whiff of Timmy's scent.

Only one time had someone spotted him on his journey. A small boy, no more than five, had been sitting in his booster seat in the back seat of his mother's car. As the car had stopped next to the bus, the child had become excited and continually pointed to the back of the bus directly at Rupert. Unfortunately for the child, only he could see him, the mother kept looking, but only saw the back of the bus, nothing there but a poster for the next action movie starting next week. Finally, the mother had turned around in her seat and had given the child a look that would melt steel.

"Jeffrey, now that's enough, I have no idea what you're pointing at, but I'm telling you there's nothing there." Then she stepped on the gas pedal and shot forward as traffic started to move again. "I swear, from now on I'm giving you nothing but sugar-free snacks."

Rupert smiled at the boy and tried to shrug a sorry, but then the bus turned a corner and the car was gone from his sight.

He had walked around more than half the street, only getting bits and pieces of Timmy's trail. The other smells of the city continually overrode his olfactory senses until he had finally given up and decided he had no choice but to wait at the bus station and hope the boy would eventually show up.

As he walked down the sidewalk, people parting as he went, he slowed when he heard his name being called.

In a nearby sewer grate, he saw a pair of beady, red eyes. So, walking over and kneeling down, he saw it was Rocky.

"Hey there, Rupert, where the hell have you been?" Rocky asked.

"That's a long story. The boy I'm with can't help but get into trouble. It's one thing after another with him. Why, have you seen him?"

Rocky grinned in the gloom of the sewer, his white teeth showing through the grate for Rupert to see. "Sure did, but its not all good news. He fell in with a couple of small-time drug dealers. I saw him leave with them. Haven't seen them since, but I know that kid needs to get away from them as soon as possible."

"Great, what am I supposed to do now?" Rupert asked, throwing his paws in the air in frustration.

"Now, calm down, big guy. I've got my best people looking for him, or should I say creatures. When he pops up, I'll know about it. I know everything that happens around here, I told you." He grinned a little more. "For example, I know you owe a certain somebody a twenty for information."

Rupert's eyebrows went up in surprise. "You do? Already? Wow, that just happened a few hours ago."

Rocky grunted. "That's right and I knew less than an hour after it happened, so be cool, if your boy's out there, we'll find him again."

Rupert sighed. "Okay, I hate to say it, but I'm going to go wait at the bus station. You know, if I could go back in time a few days, I think I would have turned down the assignment for this kid and none of this would ever have happened."

"Don't say that, Rupert, after all, if the kid hadn't run away, then you never would have met me." Then the eyes disappeared as Rocky retreated back into the sewer.

Rupert held his tongue, realizing there was no one there to talk to anymore, then he stood up and headed off to the bus terminal. All he could do was sit, wait and hope that one of Rocky's contacts found Timmy and soon, before something bad happened to him yet again.

*   *   *

Timmy sat on the sofa in the living room of Clarence and Slim. The two men were sitting at the kitchen table with some kind of white powder that looked a lot like baby powder to Timmy. He only watched them for a minute or so and then got bored and went back to watching television. The two men didn't have cable, but Timmy found some cartoons playing on one of the local channels. Tom and Jerry weren't his favorite cartoons, but they would do in a pinch.

The sky grew dark and in time he felt himself becoming drowsy. Just that morning he had been trapped in Susan and Charlie's house and now he found himself somewhere else. It wasn't that bad as far as he could tell, but he still wasn't able to leave…at least not if he wanted anything to happen to his mom.

Slim stood up and walked over to him as he stretched from filling small cylinders full of the powder.

"You look tired, kid, why don't you go lay down in the bed I made up for you in back. Clarence doesn't need it. Shit, he usually falls asleep on the damn couch every night after too many beers, anyway," Slim said.

Timmy nodded and stood on wobbly legs. He walked across the living room until he reached a door. Opening the door, he saw there was a small three foot hallway. Two doors on the left were bedrooms and the one on the right was a tiny bathroom with only a shower stall, a sink and a toilet.

111

Timmy picked the first door; the one Slim had shown him earlier in the day. He stepped inside the small room and looked around once more.

Clothes littered the floor to the point of disguising whether there was wood or carpeting beneath all the laundry. The walls had chipping paint and the window was frozen shut from dozens of paint jobs over the years, the layers of paint literally gluing the window to the frame.

The bed was unmade and the sheets were dirty. A small bedside table sat next to the bed, a tiny lamp and a broken digital alarm clock radio its only occupants.

Timmy sighed as he looked at his new accommodations.

At least Susan's house had been immaculate.

He was still scared, but it had now settled inside him to a quiet dread that was always with him. At least Clarence and Slim didn't seem to want to hurt him, on the contrary, from what they had told him, it seemed that they needed him very much in their present business venture.

Timmy sat on the bed, not really wanting to lie down. He had already decided to sleep with his clothes on, and after further thinking on the subject, and seeing a cockroach scurry across the floor to be lost in a hole in the far wall, he decided to keep his shoes on, as well.

He lay down in the bed, trying not to touch anything, and reached over and turned off the light.

He lay there quietly, staring up at the cracks on the ceiling while the bright lights of the city outside the window easily illuminated the room, filtering through the cracks in the torn and faded window shade.

Horns blowing, people yelling, the sounds of traffic, and the occasional screech of brakes filtered into the room from outside. He lay there listening to it all, wondering how he would ever fall asleep with all the noise.

Back in Virginia, on his quiet side-street, there was almost no sound with the exception of the stray commuter coming home late and dozens of crickets. He missed the sounds the crickets made now. In fact, he had never realized just how much he had grown accustomed to them until having to spend yet another night without them.

He placed his hands on his stomach and laced his fingers together, his breathing lost by the sounds floating in from outside.

Despite the constant noise, however, he slowly slipped into a light doze, hovering in that time when all people drifted on the edge between wakefulness and slumber, and before he had even realized it, he was fast asleep, dreaming of Rupert and hoping his friend would find him soon.

*   *   *

Hicks and Falzone pulled up in their unmarked police car and parked outside Clarence and Slim's building. It had been hours since they had left and now, with warrant in hand, Hicks prepared to finally take down the two, no-good drug dealers.

"Are you sure we should do this alone? What about more backup? Hell, it can't hurt to have a few more guys with us," Falzone said while he readjusted his bulletproof vest.

Next to him, Hicks made a disgusted face. "Screw that, I've been working on these two mooks for almost three weeks and if any one is gonna take them down, it's gonna be me. 'Sides, they're just a couple of idiots. This should be a piece of cake."

Falzone frowned. "What about weapons? How bad do you think they're armed?"

Hicks shrugged. "Hell if I know. Probably a couple of handguns, and if they're actually stupid enough to resist, well then screw it, it's their funeral."

Hicks headed for the front door of the building.

"Still, I hope they don't resist. I don't want to have to kill them," Hicks said ruefully.

"Really? How come?" Falzone asked.

"Because the paperwork is double if you end up killing the perps, no, I'd just rather wound them, but still, if you have to, shoot to kill. Don't take any chances on these low-lifes."

Falzone nodded and followed Hicks up the stairs until they were in the hallway with the door to Slims apartment only a few feet away.

A woman wearing the classic outfit of a hooker opened a nearby door and stopped cold. She knew police when she saw them, whether a badge was showing or not.

Hicks gestured with his left hand, his right still on his sidearm, which was still holstered. "Get the fuck back in there, woman, and keep quiet," he hissed.

The hooker snapped out of her shock and slammed the door on Hicks, just glad he didn't have business with her.

Hicks checked over his shoulder to see how Falzone was holding up. Though the man had been a beat cop, this was his first raid, and Hicks could only hope the young detective would keep his cool.

Falzone's forehead was beaded in sweat and his eyes were wide, but otherwise he seemed good. Hicks remembered his own first raid and how the adrenalin had made him feel invincible.

Not wanting to take any chances, Hicks stopped and turned to Falzone.

"You okay, partner?" He asked quietly.

Falzone nodded. "Yeah, Sarge, I'm cool, just a little nervous."

Hicks grinned at his partner's answer. At least the man was honest.

"That's fine, just use that nervousness to your advantage and stay sharp and you'll be fine."

By now Hicks had drawn his weapon, a police Glock. The weapon had a brand new clip. He knew this because he had personally loaded each 9mm shell into the clip and had sent the first round into the chamber. Whatever happened tonight, he felt ready for it.

His own heart beat faster under his Kevlar vest, his adrenalin pumping through his veins. No matter how many times he did this, he always got a subtle thrill and that was fine with him. If he didn't want the rush, then he would have become a school teacher or a mailman.

Double checking that the arrest warrant was in his back pocket, he stopped in front of the apartment's door, Falzone standing just a little to his side. It had already been planned in advance what they would do. Hicks would kick the door in and then take two steps into the room and drop to his knees. Falzone would stay by the doorframe, and with Hicks on the floor, he would have a clear line of fire if it came to that. While Hicks hoped it wouldn't go that far, especially with a child in the apartment, he knew with drug dealers you could never be too careful.

The sound of a television could be heard filtering through the door, and with one last glance at Falzone, he prepared to break in the door.

Pulling his badge out of his shirt and letting it dangle over his chest, he took three quick breaths, then lifted his right foot so it was just a few inches below the doorknob and lock.

"Okay, let's do this," he breathed and then kicked the door with all his weight behind it.

The door shattered like it was cardboard, hitting the wall and then sagging on its hinges. Hicks charged into the room with his weapon leading the way.

"New York Police, everyone down on the ground, now!" He yelled into the room, his gun already looking for targets.

Clarence and Slim were both sitting at the kitchen table, still cutting the drugs in preparation for Timmy to deliver the next day. While both men were surprised by the intrusion, they were both hardened criminals, and within the blink of an eye had thrown off their surprise and went into action.

Both men had weapons lying next to them on the kitchen table, and as Hicks charged in screaming, they both reached out and pulled their armaments to them. Clarence jumped up with an AK-47 in his hand, already spraying rounds toward the front door. Slim brought up a .357 Colt, and with the safety already off, proceeded to send high velocity rounds at the man standing at the doorframe.

The sound of gunfire in the room was deafening, the lamp on an end table vibrating from the concussions of the weapons, and a second later a stray round shot it to pieces, the lamp disintegrating an instant later.

The room was thrown into darkness, the light from the television barely enough to see by, let alone track targets by.

Whatever Hicks expected, this was not it. He was shocked at the amount of firepower the two drug dealers had and quickly realized he was severely outgunned. Multiple impacts hit his vest, causing him to lose focus. Each hit felt like a jackhammer had struck his chest. Bullets flew by his face and one nicked his ear, but in the chaos he barely noticed.

Then a stray bullet struck the television screen and sparks shot out of the glass tube, bathing the room in orange and white until the explosion subsided. The two black men were almost lost in the darkness and Hicks realized he was now exposed against the light from the hallway.

He continued firing, trying to make a hasty withdrawal when he felt wetness on the back of his head. With a snap of his head, he risked looking away, wanting to see how Falzone was when he realized the wetness had been his partner's blood.

Falzone was swaying on his feet, his free hand holding his neck. A round had passed through his throat, severing his carotid artery in its passing. The man was already dead, but just didn't know it yet.

"Joey, for Christ sake's, get the fuck down!" Hicks pleaded, but as he watched his partner stumble into the doorway, now fully exposed by the backlit hallway, he saw the man get stitched from groin to head with bullets. Despite the vest, the man jerked as each round struck him, the last striking the man in the temple. His head shot back and he dropped to the floor like a puppet with his strings cut.

Hicks stared in shock for one more heartbeat.

In real time all this had happened in less than two ticks of the second hand, but as Hicks watched his partner crumple to the hallway floor, it felt like a thousand years.

If Hicks had been thinking clearly, he would have thrown himself through the doorway and escape, to regroup and return with backup. He could have easily called for help and held the two men in the apartment until more men arrived.

But the detective was far from thinking clearly now.

With adrenalin pumping, and the shock of seeing his partner massacred in front of him, he stood up, and with his gun firing as fast as he could, he pulled the trigger of his weapon continuously and charged the two black men.

Both Slim and Clarence watched the crazy cop jump to his feet and charge at them. Both saw the feral look in his eyes and knew if they didn't take the man down fast, then they were both dead.

Unfortunately, they were only half-right.

With Hicks charging at both men, Clarence swung the AK-47 toward him and fired, while next to him Slim did the same.

Hicks felt the impacts one at a time, but the force of his moving body kept him charging forward. He fired three more times, the first round going wide, but the second and third striking Clarence in the chest. The wounded man was thrown backward, his hand still on the trigger of his weapon as the muzzle swung towards Slim.

Stray rounds stitched Slim's chest, causing the man to fire wildly.

As synapses stopped firing, Clarence dropped his weapon, and his eyes glazed over as death took him. Slim was dead before his body hit the dirt-carpeted floor.

Hicks stopped moving, realizing the battle was over. His breathing was heavy and he was almost deaf from all the gunfire. Suddenly, he felt weak and fell to his knees. A coughing fit overcame him and he coughed up what seemed like a pint of blood before he managed to get the coughing fit under control.

He knew he had broken ribs, and maybe internal bleeding from multiple gunshots in the chest to boot.

His vision grew dim and he fell onto his side, the pain from his body's impact on the floor enough to make him cry out. His radio crackled on his shoulder and he pulled it to him, the effort nothing but agony.

"Officer's down, need backup. Hostiles are down," he choked into the radio mike. Something was said back to him, but he couldn't make it out. All he could hear was his pulse pounding in his ears. Thump, thump, thump.

He looked down at himself and realized he'd had been shot dozens of times. Although the vest had helped, he still had countless bullet wounds in his arms and legs. Whether an artery had been severed was unknown.

He lay back and concentrated on breathing. He heard the sound of debris crunching under footsteps, and though he wanted to bring his weapon up, he just didn't have the strength and realized he was helpless. He was just too weak from blood loss.

With blurry vision, he looked up at the face of the small child the two drug dealers had brought into the apartment with them. Hicks plan had worked well. The boy had been in another room, and as he gazed down at the wounded policeman, Hicks could see the boy was unharmed.

Hicks tried to smile up at the boy and coughed a few more times.

"Hey, kid, I've come to rescue you," he said in a garbled voice.

The boy just stared, his eyes looking everywhere at once. Then he jumped over Hick's prone body, leaped over Falzone's corpse, and bolted out the door. Hicks heard his footsteps for a moment and then nothing.

He had no idea how long he lay there, but soon he could hear the distinctive sound of police and emergency sirens. The address for the warrant was on file, it wasn't hard for his fellow police to find him, plus the GPS tracker in the patrol car.

An indeterminate amount of time later to him, but was only ten minutes in reality, paramedics and police swarmed into the apartment.

Hands immediately began working on him, checking him for wounds, and an oxygen mask was placed over his nose and mouth.

That was when his awareness ended. With the scared face of the little boy at the forefront of his mind, Detective Hicks passed out from blood loss.

Years later, when he was asked to regale his fellow officers with the tale of the easy raid that had gone horribly wrong, and had almost cost him his life, he would always think back to that small boy's face. He had never seen the child again, and to his last day on earth, he always wondered if the boy had made it to safety or if he had just ended up running from the apartment to become embroiled in something even far worse than his fate would have been if Hicks had never arrived that fateful night.

*　　*　　*

Seconds after the raid began; Timmy awoke to the sound of the world exploding.

The gun blasts coming from the next room sounded like cannon balls were ripping through the small apartment.

Not knowing what to do, and too petrified to even think straight, he fell off the bed and rolled under the frame.

The bedroom was still shrouded in darkness, the door leading to the small hallway still closed. The staccato of Clarence's AK-47 had him covering his head with his hands and squeezing his eyes shut in terror. He had never heard something as loud as whatever was happening only a few feet from his cowering position.

What seemed like hours, but was in fact only minutes, passed, and the noise stopped, like a light switch being turned off. Still, Timmy laid still and quiet. His breathing pushed the dust-bunnies across the wood floor and he suddenly felt like sneezing. Not wanting whatever was in the other room to hear him, he tried to hold it in, but soon realized it was going to happen whether he wanted it to or not.

With a loud sneeze, his body bucked and he hit his head on the metal frame of the bed and bit his lip so he wouldn't cry out.

But all was quiet outside his door.

Whatever had happened appeared to be over, so with his curiosity peaked, despite being frightened, he opened the bedroom door and poked his head into the hallway. The first thing he noticed was the smell of gunpowder and something else. Timmy had never smelled a room covered with spilled and splattered blood before, and as he slowly stuck his head into the living room, his mouth dropped open in both surprise and shock.

Both Clarence and Slim were lying on the floor, dead, though at the moment Timmy had no real idea of whether that was true or not. All he knew was that the two men were horizontal and didn't seem to care that Timmy was out of his bed.

Then he saw Detective Hicks lying near the front door. As Timmy moved closer, he saw a pair of legs in the hallway. He couldn't see the rest of the body and for the moment didn't really want to. He walked over the scattered debris littering the floor and stopped next to Hicks.

He didn't know the man, but he did know what the shiny badge on his chest represented. This man was a policeman.

Timmy stood perfectly still, gazing down at the man. He could see the numerous wounds on the man's body and Hick's eyes stared up at Timmy, but seemed to be looking straight through him to see something far away.

The man said something to Timmy, but it was garbled.

Then Timmy realized the front door was wide open. He broke free of his surprise at finding the massacre, and without another glance at Hicks, dashed out of the apartment and into the hallway. He barely slowed as he saw the man in the hallway was either sleeping or dead. Timmy tried not to think about that, his mind already trying to come to grips with what he had just seen.

He ran to the stairwell and down the stairs, taking two at a time until he was on the ground floor. Running into the graffiti-covered lobby, he charged out onto the sidewalk, almost knocking over a homeless man with a shopping cart. The man slurred something at Timmy, but the boy never heard any of it, and with arms pumping, he ran down the sidewalk. After turning the far corner, he continued to run as fast as his legs would carry him.

The cool breeze from his running dried the tears falling from his eyes. The streets were full of cars and pedestrians, some of them looking like late night revelers. He dove between their bodies and kept running, all the bright lights of the city at night nearly blinding him.

He had no idea where he was running to, but he knew he wanted to get as far away from the apartment of death as he could.

With the moon looking down at the city that never sleeps, and a small boy running through its streets, Timmy kept moving until his breath came in gasps and his chest began to hurt.

He finally slowed when he approached Central Park. The trees and the manicured lawns made him feel like he was home. Not realizing that it wasn't very safe for an eight-year-old boy to enter the park at night, Timmy strode into the park with his head held high.

He knew he had run for a long time and he was very far away from Clarence and Slim's building. With the smell of the grass filling his nose, he walked over to a park bench and sat down, his legs not long enough to reach the cement of the path.

Another nearby bench was occupied by another homeless person.

With the person's body wrapped in loose clothing, Timmy didn't know if the bum was a man or a woman.

He didn't really care, actually.

He sat there watching the few people in the park as they walked by him. If any of them was curious about a small child in the park late at night, none showed their interest.

Time went by and Timmy felt himself growing drowsy again. While he didn't want to fall asleep in the park, at the moment he was plum out of ideas. He decided to just lie down for a little while and rest up, then he would leave the park and start out for his search for the bus station again.

Hopefully, he could find Rupert, and even if he couldn't, something much older than his years told him he needed to leave this city as soon as possible before something else bad happened to him.

With his head on his arm, he closed his eyes, telling himself he would rest for just a few minutes. But soon he was fast asleep, just another stray body in a park filled with hundreds of others with nowhere else to go.

Chapter Twenty-one

*T*HE SUN WAS just starting to peek its way through the trees of Central Park when Timmy began to stir.

He had slept for hours, not realizing how tired he had been. Sitting up, he stretched his arms and let out a large yawn. His stomach signaled him it was hungry and he slid off the park bench and started walking out of the park. A city worker was picking up trash and Timmy walked over to the man.

Timmy read the stitching on the man's shirt. In smooth written letters the name Eduardo was written in white thread. The white letters showed clearly against the gray shirt the man wore, and as Timmy stopped and looked up at him, Eduardo smiled.

"Good morning, young man, how are you today?" Eduardo asked with a slight Spanish accent. In truth, the man had been studying English for more than six months and felt he was getting better everyday. He tried to use English whenever possible, which was hard when all of his fellow co-workers spoke Spanish and were in no way motivated to speak anything but their native language. He never had the opportunity to talk to anyone in the park, though. Most people pretended he wasn't even there; he was like one of the statues in the park.

He was there, but yet no one actually noticed him.

So when the small boy walked over to him, he felt this would be the perfect chance to practice his English. After asking the boy how he was, he patiently waited for an answer.

Instead the boy started to cry in great big gasps and heaves as he tried to catch his breath. Eduardo was clueless. What should he do? Should he try to comfort the boy only to be accused of somehow trying to take advantage of him?

Finally, he decided to gesture to the boy to walk with him to a nearby park bench. Timmy followed and soon both man and boy were sitting next to each other. People cutting through the park on their way to work walked by them, barely seeing the two people. Most were already on cell phones or had their heads buried in newspapers. Almost all carried cups of coffee or some other beverage.

Eduardo patted the boy's arm, careful not to get to close to the child, but still wanting to appear sympathetic.

"There, there, my young friend. What is the matter? Are you lost? How can I help you this morning?"

Timmy slowed his crying and looked up at the nice man. Eduardo had a natural smile. He was a genuinely nice person and Timmy sensed it as he looked into the man's face.

"My name is Timmy Conrad and I'm on my way to my grandpa's house in Boston, but I got lost. Every time I try to get to the bus station something bad happens to me. My friend Rupert was with me and now I can't find him. Every time he tries to help me, we get separated. Now I don't know where I am and I'm hungry and I need to get to the bus station, but I don't know where it is and…and…" And then he started crying again, finally getting all his problems off his small chest.

Eduardo patted the boys shoulder and said soothing words like; "it'll be okay," and "don't worry, you'll be fine." The things one person says to another when they have no clue how to help them, but just want the other person to stop crying.

It still had the desired effect, though, and in a few minutes Timmy's tears slowed and he stopped crying, with the exception of a few sniffles.

Eduardo handed him a tissue and Timmy took it, blowing his nose and then handing it back.

Eduardo put up his hand, gesturing that he didn't want it back.

"That is okay, my young friend, you can keep it."

Timmy paused for a second, not understanding, but then pulled his arm back and placed the tissue on his lap.

"So, you are trying to get to the bus station, is that right, Timmy?" Eduardo asked.

"Uh-huh, I'm already really overdue, but my friend said he'd wait for me there."

Eduardo stood up, fixing his pants so the waist line was straight.

"Well, that's easy, Timmy. The bus station is only a few blocks away. If you want, I can bring you to the end of the park and point you in the right direction."

Timmy's eyes lit up. "Really? Oh wow, thanks, mister. That would be great."

Eduardo pointed to his name stitched on his chest.

"Mister is my father, Timmy. You can call me Eduardo."

Timmy smiled. The first time in a while. "Okay, Eduardo. When are we going to leave?"

Eduardo shrugged. "We can go now, but it might take a little longer than normal." He held up his broom and trash scooper. "On the way there, I need to pick up whatever trash we find. That's my job."

"Oh, okay. Can I help you?" Timmy asked.

"Sure, if you want, you can pick up the soda bottles and newspapers, but leave the rest to me. Sometimes there are sharp things inside the trash, like needles and stuff. I don't want you getting hurt."

"Okay, Eduardo," Timmy said and then the two of them walked away from the bench on their way to the end of the park.

Rhonda the fairy watched the small boy and the man walk away from the park bench. She had been in a nearby tree and had eavesdropped on the entire conversation. That was what she did. There wasn't that much else to do in the park when no one could see you and you were only a few inches tall.

By what she had heard, she was willing to bet everything she owned—which wasn't much—that the boy below her was Timmy, the kid that big, dopey-looking purple monster was looking for.

Flying off, she headed for the nearest sewer grate. She needed to get the word out. She had found the kid, and as soon as she passed it on to the monster grapevine, someone should be able to tell Rupert in no time.

With the sun glistening on her gossamer wings, she flew into the sky, always wary for pigeons or crows.

Chapter 22

RUPERT SAT IN a corner of the bus terminal trying not to go crazy.

All he wanted was to run out into the city and try to find Timmy, but he knew it would be foolish. There was no way he would ever find the boy by himself. He had been waiting for almost a day, and with the sun rising on another new day, he was starting to realize he just might have to face the reality that the child might never turn up again.

He was still wrestling with the idea of when would be the right time to give up and return to Monster City when he heard his name being called.

At first he wasn't quite sure if it was he that was being addressed, but as he looked around the terminal and no one else was in his immediate area, he quickly realized it must be him the lonely voice was addressing.

He stood up and started to look around for the source of the voice when the voice called out to him again.

"Over here, ya big dummy," said the voice.

Rupert started walking, trying to find where the voice was coming from.

"That's right, just keep walking and you'll see where I am," said the voice.

Rupert was across the bus terminal now, and as he approached the far wall, he heard a grunt coming from the large vent situated two-feet high on the brick wall.

He bent over and peeked inside. It was dark in the vent, but two, red, beady eyes and a large set of teeth reflected what ambient light penetrated into the small opening.

"Hi, Rocky, what's up?" Rupert asked. "Any news on my friend?"

Rocky nodded in the dark, but realizing Rupert probably couldn't see him, he grunted again.

"As a matter of fact, yes, there is news. Rhonda spotted him in the park. You know Rhonda, right?" He asked.

Rupert nodded. "She's a fairy, dresses a little trashy."

"Good, that's her, only don't let her hear you say that. Well, Rhonda saw him a little while ago. He's made friends with a city worker and he's on his way here now. Figure he'll be here in no time."

Rupert smiled. "Really? Oh wow, that's so great. I was just starting to think I might have to leave and return to Monster City."

"Yeah, well, about that. I had a buddy just come from home on rotation and it seems the head monster is on to you. The words out Rupert. The first monster to see you is to tell you to get your purple ass back home." He shifted in the vent; trying to get more comfortable. "I tell ya, I'm just glad I'm not you, and though I would have said that out of principle, anyway, I think you're in for a serious chewing out when you get back home."

Rupert leaned against the wall and sulked. He knew it had to happen sooner or later, he had just hoped it would have taken longer before the head office would catch on. But evidently someone had noticed when he hadn't returned at the end of his shift a few days ago. Of all the luck. He was finally going to be reunited with Timmy and he would have to leave the boy yet again.

A happy shout made him look up to see Timmy running into the bus terminal. He had seen Rupert and he was jumping up and down as he ran over to him.

"Rupert, I've found you!" He shrieked as he ran up to him. At the last second Rupert held up his hand to stop the boy from jumping into him. Already people were glancing at the yelling child who appeared to be alone.

"Whoa there, Timmy, calm down. I'm glad to see you, too, but if you jump at me people will see you, you have to stay incognito."

Timmy looked up into his face and blinked. "Incog…what?" He asked.

Rupert sighed. Sometimes he forgot Timmy was only eight. "It means to not be noticed; you know, sneaky."

Timmy understood that and he nodded quickly. "Oh, okay, if that was what you meant then why didn't you just say that?" Timmy asked innocently.

Rupert was about to answer when a bus's engine started up, blowing noxious exhaust into the terminal. Timmy coughed and tried to wave the fumes away from his face, but failed miserably.

Rupert turned and looked into the vent to tell Rocky thanks, but when he looked inside, the vent was empty; the monster was gone. Rupert decided it didn't really matter. He'd see Rocky sooner or later again back home or at the company Christmas party. Only what Monsters considered Christmas to be was very different than in the human realm. He would tell him thanks then.

Rupert started walking toward the idling bus with Timmy tagging along.

"Wow, Rupert, I can't believe I made it back here. You'd never guess where I've been and what I've seen."

Rupert nodded; his mind elsewhere as he tried to think of the best way to tell Timmy he had to leave. Timmy wasn't noticing as he regaled Rupert on his adventures.

"And I saw a bunch of dead guys and guns and then I went to McDonalds and then I met Eduardo, he works in the park, and he told me how to find you and here I am," he rambled happily.

Rupert nodded absently and then stopped Timmy when they had reached the back of the bus. Rupert had already seen the sign on the bus and was pleased to see it read Boston.

This was the bus Timmy needed to board so the boy could finally get to his grandfather's house. People were already climbing onto the bus and luggage was being tossed into the rear luggage compartment.

Rupert knelt down on his knees so he was eye to eye with Timmy.

"Look, Timmy, I have some bad news. I'm afraid I need to go home now. I can't go the rest of the way with you."

"What, but why?" Timmy asked.

"Because my boss back home found out I was gone and I need to get back there. Hopefully, I can talk my way out of anything serious and before you know it, I'll be back with you," Rupert said.

"You promise?" Timmy asked.

Rupert grinned and nodded yes, his fangs showing clearly. Timmy barely noticed. To him, Rupert wasn't a monster, but someone who was his friend and cared for him. Since his father had died, Timmy had been in short supply of those and he started to cry when he realized his friend was leaving him.

"But I don't want you to go; we're a team," he said softly, trying to keep the tears at bay, but failing miserably. "You're supposed to protect me from David."

Rupert patted his shoulder and tried to hold his smile, but his emotions gave him away.

"I know that, pal, but I have no choice." He pointed to the bus. "Now, listen, I want you to go over to the stairs of the bus and walk up them. You can't cry; you have to look like it's no big deal to be getting on that bus. If the bus driver asks you for a ticket, you tell him your mom's in the bathroom and she has the tickets and she'll be right out. If bus drivers are the same here as back home, then by the time he's ready to leave, he'll have forgotten all about you, so just pick a seat in the back and stay quiet."

Timmy nodded, sniffling. "Okay, Rupert, but you better come back to me," he warned and started moving towards the bus.

Rupert waved. "Don't you worry, when you need me the most, I'll be there for you, I promise."

Timmy was at the door to the bus now, and with one last glance over his shoulder, he stepped into the rumbling vehicle. The bus driver's nose was buried in a newspaper and he never looked up while Timmy boarded. Timmy moved passed him and picked a seat in the back. The large seat was huge to the boy and he felt smaller than ever.

The people around him talked to each other or read the paper. Some were on cell phones. One teenager was listening to music with a set of headphones. Even with the headphones on, Timmy could hear the music clearly. He winced, imagining how loud the music must be and mentally told himself he would never listen to music that loud when he grew older.

Looking out the window, he saw Rupert standing on the sidewalk. He waved to the monster and Rupert waved back. His heart was heavy and he missed his friend already. The engine surged with power and the air brakes hissed as the driver prepared to leave the bus station.

With a loud slap, the doors were closed and the bus started forward. Timmy placed his hand on the glass and watched as Rupert fell away from his vision, until he was lost behind the bus.

He sighed to himself. He was alone again, but at least he was finally on his way to see his grandpa.

He shifted to a better position in his seat and looked out the window as the bustling city flew by him. All the people were still going about their business, barely aware of each other. Timmy had learned a lot since he had left home only a few days ago. While he may have only been eight years old, he felt like he had aged at least double in the busy city of New York.

Thirty minutes later, the bus broke free of the gridlock and finally pulled onto the interstate. Other than a few other stops in Connecticut and Rhode Island, Timmy was finally on his way to Boston, and though he missed Rupert terribly, he knew he had to stand on his own two feet.

After all, that was what his father would have wanted him to do if he hadn't died and was still with him.

With a weary sigh, he leaned back in his seat and tried to get comfortable for the last leg of his journey.

Rupert watched the bus pull out of the terminal and his heart broke. He had really taken a liking to the small child and would miss him terribly. With a slight sigh, he headed out of the bus terminal.

Now he needed to find the nearest portal home.

He wasn't worried, though, as he should be able to find one in short order. Either Rocky, Rhonda or one of the hundreds of other monsters inhabiting New York could steer him to the closest one.

With a weight in his heart that he knew he needed to throw off, he walked out onto the streets of New York.

The head monster was waiting and he was definitely not looking forward to it.

*   *   *

David tried to get more comfortable as he sat quietly in his car watching Timmy's grandparent's house. He had arrived more than a day ago and had still seen no sign of the little bastard. He grumbled to himself, his mood growing fouler with every second that ticked by.

He needed a shower and he was getting tired of having to pee in a cup, but that was how a stakeout worked, and while he was no policeman, he had seen more than enough cop shows to know this was how it was done.

The second he left to get a shower or tried to grab something to eat, that would be when Timmy would arrive.

No, he thought, if he ever wanted to dig himself out of the mess he'd made for himself, then he'd have to wait for Timmy and head the boy off before he could contact his grandparents.

He was parked a few houses down from the home he was watching and for the tenth time a woman with a dog walked by and gave him a dirty look. He decided right then that if he didn't diffuse the situation, then the woman would probably end up calling the cops on him, thinking he was some kind of Peeping Tom or a child snatcher.

Rolling down his window, he gave her his sincerest smile.

"Hi, there, I've seen you walk by a few times before, can I help you with anything?" He asked pleasantly.

She frowned and moved a few feet to his window, but stopped before she would be within arms reach. The dog continued to pull on its leash, wanting to keep moving. There were far too many trees and fences to mark to slow down now.

"Actually, you can," she said. "Just who are you and what are you doing on my street. I've seen you here for more than a day now. You can't blame me for being curious."

David nodded, trying to think up a decent excuse to get the woman to layoff. Then an idea struck him and he ran with it.

"Umm, I'm a private investigator. See that house over there? Well, the guy who lives there is collecting workman's compensation and we think he's lying. I'm here to catch him doing yard work or something physical so we can get his case dismissed."

The woman's face lightened, the devious part of her showing through. She was now in on something interesting.

"Really? You know, I always had a feeling they were up to something. They're just too nice, and you know what they say about people that are too nice. Don't you?"

He didn't and said so. "No ma'am, I don't."

She leaned in closer as if he was a fellow conspirator. "They say they usually have something to hide."

David just stared at her, not really knowing what to say. The woman stood back up and realized she needed to go before her dog started to drag her away.

"Your secrets safe with me, I won't say a word," she said.

"Thank you, ma'am. Now, could I ask you to move along? I wouldn't want my cover to be blown by me talking to you."

"Oh, of course not, silly me. Well, goodbye then," she said and started off down the street, the dog happily moving once more.

David let out a breath and sighed. That was close, he thought. He leaned back in his seat and grinned to himself. He couldn't believe he was able to fool that nosy woman into thinking he was a private investigator. Maybe he was a better actor than he thought.

With the woman gone it was back to watching the house again. He sighed, suffering the seconds as they ticked by excruciatingly slowly.

The little brat had to show up soon, he just had to, because if he didn't, David was all out of ideas.

With the sun glaring off his windshield, he turned on the air conditioning and tried for the thousandth time to get more comfortable.

Chapter Twenty-three

*T*IMMY WATCHED THE rolling landscape drift by while the bus drove down the highway. He could almost imagine he was flying and the plane was just drifting a few feet above the ground.

After a while, the view became the same, nothing but trees and grass.

He drifted off into a light sleep and was awakened a short time later by another passenger on the bus.

An older woman in her late sixties was opening a sandwich wrapped in aluminum foil, the wrapper crinkling softly.

Timmy opened one eye and watched her, silently. As she took a bite of the sandwich, he felt his own stomach begin to rumble. He hadn't eaten since the night before and he was now starving again. He sat up, wiping sleep from his eyes and watched the woman as she took another bite of her sandwich.

The woman chewed softly, and when her eyes caught Timmy staring, she smiled.

"Well, hello there, honey. Are you hungry? You're eyeing me like a fox in a henhouse."

Timmy looked down, embarrassed.

"Oh, that's okay. I was just joking. Are you hungry?"

Timmy nodded. "Yes I am. I haven't had anything to eat since yesterday."

"Oh, you poor thing, here, have some of my sandwich. Do you like egg salad?"

She asked while handing him the other half of the sandwich.

Timmy took it and started eating ravenously. He just nodded as he ate.

The woman grinned. By the way the boy was eating, he very obviously liked egg salad.

In less then a minute, Timmy had finished the sandwich and was looking back at her. While the worst of his hunger was sated, he was still very hungry. It was like the half sandwich had only pacified the hungering beast and in a very short time the beast would awaken again even more ravenous than before.

While Timmy was still hungry, he was hesitant to ask for more. With the exception of Eduardo, who had helped him back to the bus station, every time he met an adult they ended up wanting to hurt him.

The woman seemed to sense his discomfort and smiled at him, then she reached into the large purse on her lap and pulled out a small bag of potato chips.

With her smile still on her face, she offered the bag of chips to Timmy.

"Would you like these, too, honey? I really shouldn't eat them anyway, there's too much salt in them. Bad for the blood pressure."

Timmy had no idea what she was talking about, but food was food. He took the bag, and after ripping it open, devoured the contents in due time.

While he ate, the woman asked him a few questions. Where was he going and was he alone? How come he wasn't with an adult?

Timmy answered as best he could without telling too much. By the time he had finished the chips, the woman's curiosity was satisfied and she went back to reading an old paperback book she had pulled from her voluminous purse.

Timmy finished sucking the crumbs from the bottom of the bag and then left his seat to go to the bathroom.

Once he was inside the small room, he used his hand as a cup and drank quickly from the small faucet. Then deciding that if he was already there, he might as well use the facilities. Every time the bus would hit a bump in the road, Timmy had to protect his head from hitting the wall.

Finally, when he was finished, he went back to his seat. The woman was still reading and only glanced up to smile at Timmy once more.

Timmy smiled back and then sat back down. As he looked out the window of the bus, he started to see more and more residential homes. Buildings started to appear, large structures, housing businesses and warehouses.

If he was right, then they were getting closer every second. His heart started beating faster as he tried to think what he was going to tell his grandpa, but despite that, he was still excited. He hadn't seen his grandparents in almost a year; David banning them from seeing him.

Thinking of David made him restless. He wondered what his step-dad was doing right now back in Virginia.

He bet he must be really pissed off once he'd found out Timmy had run away. That made him think of his mother and an aching consumed his heart.

He missed her terribly, and though he would like to call home and tell her he was all right, he knew he had to wait until he was safe at his grandparent's house.

Only then would he be safe from David's wrath.

With the bus rocking back and forth as the bus driver entered heavier traffic, Timmy slumped in his seat.

Though he was frightened about what would come next, his resolve was firm. He would make it to his grandparent's house and tell them everything. After that it was out of his hands.

*　　*　　*

Stepping off the portal platform, Rupert let out a joyful sigh. No matter what the reason he had for returning to Monster City, after the past couple of days on Earth it felt good to be home.

The monster on the portal controls, a round, green looking ball of fur, smiled at Rupert as he looked up from his control board.

"Tough assignment?" The worker asked.

Rupert chuckled at the question. "Buddy, you have no idea." Then he stretched his muscles and headed for the door.

He had an appointment with the head monster and he knew better than to keep the creature waiting.

Stepping out into the light of the day, he felt at ease. Though Monster City resembled New York in countless ways, it still felt wonderful to be able to interact with every single creature he came upon, not just a select few.

A giant red and yellow vehicle was slowly working its way down the street, its bottom half hugging the curb. The street sweeper left the road behind it crystal clean, the harsh scrubbers doing a fantastic job of scraping up any dirt or refuse.

Rupert felt a pang of loss as he watched the sweeper pass him by. The driver noticed Rupert and figured he was just admiring his machine, but Rupert was once again reminded of Timmy and their trip to New York.

While multi-colored, the sweeper resembled the ones he had seen in New York as he had waited for Timmy to return to the bus station.

He wondered now if the boy was all right, hoping he had made it to Boston without anymore problems.

As for Rupert, he had his own problems to attend to. So, setting off down the wide sidewalk, headed to the main office.

He stopped at a small food cart bordering the edge of the street, and after pulling out a couple of multi-colored rats, he bought himself a sandwich. After days of being in his pocket, the rats had died and he wasn't able to get full market value for them, but considering his position, the food vendor had treated him well.

There were many creatures in Monster City that preferred their food dead and rotting, but the less talked about them the better.

Rupert continued on his way and in less than a half hour was once again in front of the large building for monster affairs.

Stepping into the wide lobby, he watched all the different monsters coming and going.

Once again he felt good to be home.

Riding the elevator to the second floor, he stepped out and was soon opening the door to the head monster's office.

The secretary, a large millipede-like creature, waved him through.

"Go right in, sir, he's been waiting for you," she said, while her sixteen arms did multiple things at the same time. The Secrepedes, as they were called, were the ideal secretary, able to multi-task dozens of chores at the same time.

Rupert gulped and did as he was directed.

Stepping into the office, Cecil looked up from his desk. Cecil's tail waved back and forth behind him as if the monster was agitated. He placed the pen he had been writing with onto his large desk and then leaned forward, folding his hands in front of him.

"Hello, Rupert, I think you have some explaining to do," he hissed. "Sit down and tell me all about it, will you?"

Rupert sat down, his eyes staring at the floor. He had no idea what he could possibly say to Cecil that would not get him into trouble and reassigned to the lowest work a monster could do; a job so low to even think about it was bad luck.

Rupert quickly tried to think of something else, hoping he had chased the subject from his mind in time.

"Well, my boy, I'm waiting."

Rupert sighed, realizing he was screwed. He decided to just tell the truth. He started from the beginning and how he had escorted Timmy to New York and had then helped him escape a house by setting it on fire. He told Cecil about Rocky and Rhonda and how he had lost the boy when he had climbed onto a pickup truck. He finished by telling Cecil that when he had heard he was summoned home, he had immediately returned, leaving the boy to fend for himself.

Through the entire story, Cecil never said a word, only nodding every now and then. His phone had rung once and he had simply told his secretary to hold his calls, then had bid Rupert to continue.

When Rupert was finished, he leaned back in his chair and just looked at Rupert.

If Rupert could sweat, he would have been perspiring buckets, he was so nervous.

Finally, Cecil sat up straight and slapped the top of his desk.

"Wonderful, what an amazing story! You are quite a brave soul to risk what you have risked and all for one small boy."

Rupert said nothing, more than a little surprised by Cecil's take on the subject.

Cecil stood up and walked over to the wall of awards.

"I'm going to let you in on a little secret, Rupert. Some of these awards on the wall are not all they appear to be. I, too, have made friends with the human children and it was they that helped me get some of my awards. You see, some humans are more insightful than others and they are the ones that see right through us and know what we are."

"And what is that, sir?" Rupert asked.

"That we're just like them. We have feelings and needs and that we love. Did you ever wonder why we scare the human children and infiltrate their world like we do?

Rupert shook his head no.

"Exactly. We have been doing this for so damn long, no one even remembers why we do it. And that's where you come in, Rupert."

"I do?"

"Yes, you do. You proved that we have free will, that we don't have to do the same thing day after day. We could leave the humans alone and work to better our own world. Do you have you any idea the kind of resources it takes to power that portal?"

Rupert shrugged. "Not really, sir, no. All that is a little beyond me."

"Maybe so, my boy, but when push came to shove, you did what your gut told you to do. That shows promise. I want to change things in Monster City and I have been patiently waiting for a few good creatures to do it with me." He stood in front of Rupert and grinned. "What do you say, Rupert? Are you with me?"

Rupert was shocked. Out of all the scenarios he had thought about on his way to the head office, this was the last one he would have guessed.

"Umm, yes?" Rupert said, not quite sure, but sensing that was the answer Cecil was looking for.

Cecil clapped his massive claw-like hands in front of him and sat back down.

"Wonderful, this is wonderful. Now all this is of course to be kept hush, hush. I don't want to spring it on the residents of the city until I'm good and ready and that could take months, if not years. How does that sit with you?"

Rupert's head was spinning. "Umm, fine I guess."

"Good, that's good. Now the first thing is to get you an office in this building. You'll have a few people under you and I want you to keep an eye out for others like yourself, creatures that aren't afraid to push the line, so to speak."

Rupert thought back to New York and both Rocky and Rhonda came to mind. They had both shown initiative and he already knew them. Plus, he owed them big. Now would be his chance to pay them back.

"I already think I might have a few candidates, sir," he said.

"Wonderful, that's wonderful. All right then, why don't you take some time off and I'll see you tomorrow, bright and early."

Rupert stood up and was about to leave. But he hesitated. Cecil saw his face and knew there was something Rupert wanted to say, but was holding back.

"Go on, out with it. I can see you want to ask me something."

Rupert nodded and with a heavy sigh, leaned on Cecil's desk.

"I want to go back one more time and see how Timmy's doing. He should be at his grandparent's house, so the portal could be sent to one of the home's bedrooms. That will be where the boy will be sleeping. After all he's been through; I just want to make sure he's safe."

Cecil mulled it over for a few moments and then waved him away.

"Fine, fine, just get it over with so we can get on to business. We have a lot to do, you and me."

Rupert smiled, a sense of relief flooding through him. "Yes, sir and thank you, sir."

Cecil waved his thanks away, already talking on the phone on a business call.

Rupert left the room, and with a polite wave to the secretary, headed out of the office and back to the street.

He wanted to take a quick detour by his apartment. He needed a good washing up and he wanted to grab something more to eat. Then he was planning on stopping by the Professor's to see what he was up to.

Then it was off to see Timmy one final time.

Chapter Twenty-four

THE BUS PULLED into South Station in the middle of Boston and with a jerking halt, then finally stopped. Air brakes hissed as the bus driver engaged the emergency brake and turned off the engine.

The steady drone of the motor ceased and passengers began to disembark.

The older woman next to Timmy gathered her belongings, and with one last smile, stood up and started down the aisle.

Timmy was the last off the bus. He looked around the station, not quite sure what to do next.

He couldn't call his grandparents, not knowing their number, so he decided to see if a cab would take him there.

Walking out of the bus station, he stopped and surveyed his surroundings. The Treasury building stood tall and grand just across the busy street from where Timmy gawked.

Similar to New York, people moved past him and around him, barely noticing an eight-year-old boy standing alone on the streets of Boston.

He started walking down the street, his eyes looking everywhere at once. To him, Boston was a lot like New York with the exception the buildings weren't so big and the streets were smaller, but other than that, he guessed one city was as good as another.

Reaching the end of the street, he noticed a line of taxi cabs idling on the corner. Picking up his pace, he jogged over to the last one in line. He was about to ask the driver something when the man pointed to the front of the line. Timmy didn't understand at first, but then realized the driver wanted him to go to the first cab in line. Walking down the street, he finally stopped at the head cab.

A middle aged man wearing a plaid shirt and a week's worth of stubble sat in the driver's seat. In his hands were the remains of a sandwich, although most of it seemed to have landed in his lap.

Timmy knocked on the passenger window and waited for the driver to see him. The man did, but when he saw it was only a small boy, he frowned.

Looking aggravated, he lowered the window and stared at Timmy, his eyes showing clear annoyance.

"Listen, kid, whatever you're selling, I don't want any."

At first Timmy didn't understand what the man meant, but then he realized the man thought he was some kind of Boy Scout selling cookies or magazines.

"No, you don't understand. I need a ride to my grandpa's house. Can you take me there?"

"Aren't you a little young to be running around here all alone? Shouldn't you be in school or something?" The cab driver asked.

Timmy shrugged, not having an answer. "Listen, mister, I really need to get to my grandpa's, could you take me there? Please?"

The driver looked over his shoulder and around the street, hoping another credible customer would arrive so he could leave this weird kid behind, but it was a beautiful day and most people were walking; Boston being a walking city.

The driver sighed. "You got any money? You know, cab rides aren't free."

Timmy shook his head. "I lost all my money, but once we get to my grandpa's house I'm sure he'll pay you. Please?" Timmy lay on the puppy eyes, hoping the driver was a soft touch like his own dad used to be before he died.

The driver sighed heavily and cursed something under his breath. Timmy had no way of knowing the cab driver had three kids of his own. Looking at the small boy, he knew he would help the child, after all, what if it was one of his own children who needed help?

"Fine, kid, get in, and so help me if, I don't get paid when we arrive, there's gonna be hell to pay," he said, grumpily.

Timmy smiled and climbed into the front seat. The driver was about to tell him to get in back, but decided to just screw it. His youngest son was almost the same age as Timmy, and though he'd hate to admit it, he felt bad for the kid, though not bad enough to waste an hour round trip bringing the kid home.

"Hey, kid, you need to buckle up. I don't need a ticket."

Timmy saw the seatbelt and clicked it into its matching buckle.

The cabby pulled into traffic, and when he was safely in the right lane, he glanced over at Timmy and asked: "So where are we going, kid? You've got an address right?"

Timmy thought for a second, trying to remember the Christmas cards he would make and address to his grandparents only a year before. Then his eyes lit up when the address came to him.

"They live in Stoneham, Massachusetts. Do you know where that is?"

"Sure I do, but I need a house address. Stoneham is a big place, kid."

"Oh, sorry, they live on Chestnut Street, but I don't remember the number of the house."

The driver turned onto Route 93 and headed out of the city.

"Have you been there before? Would you recognize the house if you saw it?" The cabby asked.

Timmy nodded animatedly. "Oh, sure, I used to go there all the time, there's a small store where you can buy milk and candy and stuff on the corner and their house is half-way down the street. Me and my grandpa used to walk there to get eggs and stuff when I spent time there in the summer."

That made Timmy ache inside, thinking of all the summer days he would spend with his grandparents. His parents would drive down from Virginia and stay a day or so, then they would leave him there. He always had a lot of fun playing in the big backyard and going to the circus at the Boston Garden. His grandpa would bring him every year. He would go to the movies with him and sometimes they would just go for a walk together and talk about stuff. His grandma was cool, too, but it was his grandfather that really loved children. Heck, he even read comic books and watched cartoons, just like a regular kid.

As Timmy thought about him, he realized he had to be one of the coolest grandpas in the world.

The cab drove for a little more than ten minutes before Timmy saw signs for Stoneham. The large green and white signs hung over the highway and Timmy pointed at the first one he saw with Stoneham on it.

"Is that the one? Is that where we're going?"

The cabby nodded, and though devoid of a signal to the other vehicles on the road, he took the exit. Timmy watched the world go by his window, marveling at all the houses. It started to remind him of back home.

Quaint houses with manicured lawns lined the roads; grass and trees on the sidewalks. The streets were clean, as well, and there was barely any debris in the gutters that he could see as the cab drove further into the small city.

Finally, the cab slowed and the driver pointed to a small convenience store.

"Look there, kid, this is Chestnut Street and there's a store. Does it look familiar?"

Timmy looked out his window and tried to remember if he was in the right place. His forehead wrinkled in concentration and he started to bite his lip.

Finally, the cabby grew impatient.

"Well, is it or isn't it the right one?"

Timmy was about to say he wasn't sure when he saw the house next to it. The house itself wasn't very memorable, but the big tree on the front lawn brought back memories of him running from his grandpa and hiding behind the tree as they played on one of their many trips to the store.

Timmy turned to look at the cabby and pointed his finger down the street.

"Go that way, mister. My grandpa's house is down there."

The driver did as he was told, mumbling something about getting screwed out of a fare. The cab rolled slowly down the street, and the more Timmy saw the houses, the more that came back to him.

Less than two minutes later he called a halt.

"Stop, stop here, that's my grandpa's house!" He called and tried to jump out of the cab while it was still moving. The cabby hit the brakes just before Timmy fell out. Timmy ran from the cab and up the walkway, jumping the three stairs that led to the small front porch.

Ringing the bell, he continued pressing the button until he heard noise from inside the house.

His grandpa opened the door, an angry look on his face, ready to give the rude person ringing his bell a piece of his mind, when his mouth fell open in shock.

"What the…Timmy? What in all the world are you doing here?"

Timmy jumped into his grandpa's arms, nearly knocking the older man over.

William Conrad, Billy to his friends, was still in good shape for just hitting the big seven-o, but his seventy year old frame couldn't take the weight of Timmy plowing into him so suddenly. He staggered backward and leaned against the wall, dropping Timmy to the floor. Timmy let his feet hit the floor, but he never let go of his grandpa

"Oh, Grandpa, I made it, you don't know how happy I am to see you!" Timmy said, hugging him tightly.

Before Billy could ask another question, a loud horn sounded from outside in the street. Timmy moved away from Billy and pointed to the cab.

"I'm really sorry, Grandpa, but I had to ride in a cab to get here from the bus station. I didn't have any money and I told that man that you would pay him."

Billy's eyes went wide in surprise.

"Oh really, well then I guess I'll have to go pay him."

Billy stepped outside and walked down the walkway. He was in his socks, but didn't seem to mind.

Timmy waited on the porch as Billy talked to the driver for a few seconds and then reached into his pocket, pulling out what Timmy guessed was money.

Billy handed the driver enough to make him happy because an instant after taking the money, the cab pulled away from the curb and sped off back the way he'd come.

Billy walked back up the walkway, a smile on his face.

"That damn cab ride cost me forty bucks, Timmy."

"Sorry, Grandpa," Timmy apologized.

Billy chuckled. "That's okay, son."

For the first time he realized Timmy was alone.

"Timmy, where are your parents? Where's your mother?" He made a face and asked: "And where's David?"

Timmy shrugged shyly. "I don't know, I guess she's back home. As for David…" He trailed off.

"Back home? Well then, how the hell did you get here from Virginia?" In the excitement of seeing his grandson, he hadn't heard Timmy tell him about the bus a few minutes ago.

Timmy lowered his head and stared at his feet. "I took a bus," he said softly.

"You did what? All the way from Virginia? Timmy, that's very dangerous. Do you have any idea how many bad people are out there just waiting to take advantage of a small boy like you?"

Timmy grinned casually. "Well, actually…" He started to say, thinking of his adventures in New York, but Billy stopped him and pulled him close, hugging him tightly.

"Forget it, Timmy, it doesn't matter now. You're here and you're safe. Just promise me you'll never do such a foolish thing like that again."

Timmy nodded. "Okay, Grandpa, never again."

"Good, now let's go call your mother. She must be worried sick." He closed the front door and ushered Timmy into the kitchen. "You hungry, boy?"

"Yes, Grandpa, I'm starving."

"All right then, your grandma's away for the next two days, but I guess I can rustle you up a sandwich or two. She's on one of them cruises with her sister. They get to gamble and stuff. I don't go in for all that, so I let her go without me. God bless her, but it's nice to have the place to myself, even if it's just for a few days." He winked at Timmy. "Get to walk around in my underwear and there's no one to yell at me."

Timmy chuckled at that and smiled, sitting down at the kitchen table. But then his face grew serious.

"Grandpa, I have some things to tell you, some bad things. That's why I came here to see you."

Billy sat down next to him and placed a bologna sandwich in front of each of them.

"Can it wait until after we eat? Or do you need to talk about it now. It's up to you, Timmy? You know I'm here for you, son."

Timmy looked down at the sandwich and his mouth watered and his stomach heaved in hunger.

"No, I guess it can wait until later; eating's good for now."

Billy grinned at his grandson. "All right then, dig in."

Both of them ate heartily, and once Timmy was finished, Billy made him another sandwich and Timmy washed both down with three large glasses of lemonade. He hadn't eaten this good since the two black men had brought him to McDonalds.

With his stomach satisfied, Timmy and Billy talked well into the day and Timmy started to feel better. He was finally safe, his pilgrimage finished.

When Billy pulled out a fresh apple pie and offered him a slice, Timmy thought he had died and gone to Heaven.

Slowly, his troubles were forgotten and he just enjoyed being an eight-year-old kid with his grandfather.

*   *   *

Outside on the street, only a few houses down from Billy's, David watched the cab disappear in the distance.

Finally, after waiting for days, Timmy had arrived. His gamble had paid off and the boy had come to him.

At first he was just going to charge into the house and demand his step-son back, but quickly dismissed the idea as reckless.

Instead, he decided to wait until dark.

Once the boy was asleep, he could break a window and sneak into the house and take care of the little brat once and for all.

In the morning when Billy would wake up to find the boy's body, it would be him who would have to explain to the police how his grandson had made it all the way from Virginia and had wound up dead in his home.

It was perfect.

David started the car and drove away. Now that he knew where Timmy was, he could go rent a room and get cleaned up. A long hot shower and a good meal would be just the thing after spending long days sitting in his car.

With a sinister smile on his face, he turned the corner and started searching for a motel or something similar.

Darkness was only a few short hours away, and when the day had finally ended and the light was gone from the sky, so too would all his problems disappear like the sun setting on the horizon.

CHAPTER TWENTY-FIVE

*R*UPERT ENTERED THE lobby to his apartment building and promptly slipped on a slime trail left by Ralph the doorman.

His legs flew out from under him and he fell hard, striking his head on the floor. He groaned from pain.

Ralph slid into view and reached down to help him up.

"Oh my, by the Great Creator, Rupert, are you all right? I'm so sorry, I was just going to get a mop and clean this up. When I get nervous, I leave a messy trail behind myself. I didn't realize I had made it until only a few minutes ago."

Rubbing his head with his hand, Rupert frowned. "Well, you could have put up a sign or something," he said.

"Umm, sorry, but I did." Ralph pointed to a yellow sign that stood in the middle of the lobby. Similar to a wet floor sign from Earth, this sign had the picture of a snail and a slime trail with the words Beware stenciled on it in black script.

"I had to put that there or I'd risk a lawsuit if someone fell." He grinned shamelessly at Rupert. "Like you."

Still rubbing his head, Rupert started to move toward the elevators. "Well, next time, maybe you could put one closer to the door before I step into the lobby," he said with the emphasis on the word: before.

Ralph nodded agreeably. "Sure, Rupert, not a problem. Hope you're okay."

Rupert waved his answer, and with the opening of the elevator doors, stepped inside.

Elevator music played softly as the car rode downward, the numbers flickering as each floor was passed. Finally, the car stopped and he stepped out onto his floor.

Walking softly down the hallway, he started humming the tune from the elevator.

"Great, now I can't get that stupid song out of my head," he muttered as he reached his apartment door.

Just before he could open his door and slip inside, the door across the hall from him opened and Mrs. Mellanger stepped out. She had a look on her face like she had already caught her prey and just wanted to play with it for a while before devouring it.

"Why, hello, Rupert. I haven't seen you in a few days. Been on assignment?" She purred.

Rupert was not in the mood for her games, but as she was larger than him and could actually eat him if she so chose, he decided politeness would win the day.

"Hello, Mrs. Mellanger; yes, I've been on assignment. Missed me?"

"You know it, handsome. What do you say you come into my place and I'll make you something to eat? A growing boy like you must always be hungry," she cooed softly.

Rupert turned to look at her.

Her white lingerie was covered in red splotches. It was either ketchup or blood and Rupert highly doubted it was ketchup. He was able to see around her body into her apartment and his heart skipped a beat when he saw what was behind her.

From his vantage point, the couch was in plain view as well as the motionless leg of a brown monster that lay sprawled on the floor at an unnatural angle.

"Umm, well, it looks like you already have company," Rupert stated, hiding his nervousness nicely.

Mrs. Mellanger looked over her shoulder and then shrugged. "Him? He was barely an appetizer, now you, my boy. Well, that's a full course meal."

Rupert slid the key into his front door with his hands behind his back. When the door popped inward, he slowly started retreating until he was ready to slip inside his apartment.

"Ah gee, Mrs. Mellanger, I'd love to, but I need to take a rain check. I need to get back to Earth. I just stopped by here to take a shower and grab a few things, then I'm gone again. Rain check?" He asked, smiling with his most sincere smile.

The wind went out of her and she frowned. "Oh, very well, but I'm holding you to it. The second you get back."

Rupert nodded, and then with his body fully in his apartment, he waved quickly and closed the door. A moment later he heard the click of Mrs. Mellanger's door closing, too.

He leaned against his door and let out the breath he'd been holding. After he had regained his composure, he went about the few chores in the apartment he needed to accomplish before leaving again.

When he was finished, he pocketed a few colorful rats for currency, the little rodents arguing the entire time, and quietly left the apartment.

As he snuck down to the elevator, hoping his neighbor wouldn't hear him, he mentally decided it was time to move to another building.

He really had no choice in the matter.

It was apparently clear his health depended on it.

*   *   *

With night falling, both Timmy and Billy were preparing for a night of watching television and spending time together.

It had been hours since Timmy had arrived and the phone call to his mother was now pleasantly in the past.

His mom had sounded more lucid than usual and had been relieved to hear he was okay. Billy had inquired about David, but she'd said she had no idea where he'd gone off to.

That was fine with Billy.

Since his own son had died, Billy had missed him terribly, taking the loss hard.

When Timmy's mother had decided to remarry, it had been yet another blow. With a new husband on her arm it was almost like his son was being replaced.

His heart ached when he looked at Timmy, seeing his late son staring back at him.

Timmy had his father's eyes and jaw, and despite the fact Billy was upset that the boy had traveled all the way from Virginia alone, it also made him smile.

His late son had the same kind of will. A determination to do something no matter how difficult or dangerous.

True, his son may be dead, but his boy's spirit lived on in his grandson.

Timmy's mom had said she would leave in the morning to come get Timmy. Billy had told her to take her time, so he could enjoy some quality time with his grandson.

Now the two of them sat on the couch together, watching a rerun of M.A.S.H. Though Timmy didn't quite get the show's jokes, he still chuckled whenever Billy did.

He had almost forgotten what it felt like to spend time with him. Billy was an adult, but yet he liked a lot of the same things Timmy did. He even knew what Yu-Gi-Oh and Pokemon was, something his own parents had been clueless about for years.

The night continued and Billy noticed Timmy was yawning. Billy copied him, sending out a loud yawn that sliced into the silence in the house.

"Wow, cut it out, Timmy, you know that's contagious."

"Sorry, Grandpa, I guess I'm ready to go to bed."

Billy stood up; setting the blanket he had across his legs to the side.

"All right, sport, right this way, your room awaits."

Timmy slid off the couch and followed Billy through the short hallway to the back of the house. Three doors were at the end, one was Billy's room, the other a bathroom, and the third was a guest room.

At one time it had been Timmy's father's room, but years ago Billy had transformed it into a guest room for Timmy and his sister-in-law. She had moved to California and would fly down and visit every now and then.

That was always torture for Billy, having two women in the house gabbing for days on end, always within earshot. During those visits, he usually found himself taking a lot of walks. If his wife noticed, she never let on.

Billy opened the door to the guestroom and Timmy stepped inside.

"Well, how is it?" Billy asked.

"Its fine, Grandpa. A lot better than some of the places I've slept lately."

"Oh? And where might that have been?"

Timmy shrugged. "Never mind, Grandpa, it doesn't matter." He turned and gave his grandfather a big hug. "Nothing matters now that I'm here."

Billy rubbed Timmy's hair with his hand and grinned.

"I'm glad you're here, too." Then his face lit up as he remembered something Timmy had said when he had first arrived.

"Timmy, when you first showed up, you said you wanted to talk to me about something. Something important. Do you want to talk about it now?"

Timmy held back a yawn and shook his head. All his troubles seemed a million miles away now that he was safe with his grandfather.

"No, its okay, we can talk about it tomorrow. I'm pretty tired now."

Billy rubbed his hair some more and then turned to leave.

"Okay, son, if you need anything I'm just across the hall. Night."

"Goodnight, Grandpa, I love you," Timmy said.

Billy stopped at the door and smiled. "I love you to, Timmy. I'm still upset that you came here alone, but I'm glad you're here. I missed you."

Timmy smiled back as he started to pull off his shirt and get ready for bed.

"I missed you, too, Grandpa, that's why I came."

Billy waved one last goodnight and then closed the door with a soft click, then moved off to his own bedroom to get ready for bed. He planned on making himself a bowl of ice-cream and then taking it to bed and watching television in his room until sleep finally came.

He chuckled softly. His wife would have killed him for eating in bed, but she wasn't here now and he was seventy for Heaven's sake, he should be able to do what he wanted.

With his slippers sliding on the hardwood floor, he went about his chores before retiring to bed, while Timmy finished taking off his clothes, and with nothing but his underwear on, slipped into the cool sheets of the bed.

Outside, crickets sang their night songs and nearby homes went dark as the occupants retired for the night.

A crescent moon gave off a feeble yellow light, bathing the town of Stoneham in its glow as the small city went to sleep at the end of a long day.

Hours later, after night had fully blanketed the city, two headlights pierced the darkness and slowed to a stop in front of Billy's house. The street was quiet, not even the sound of a dog barking its displeasure at being left outside to mar the silence.

The driver's side door opened on the car and a pair of shoes stepped out onto the cooling asphalt. The car door was closed gently, as if the driver was doing his best to remain unnoticed.

Then the dark figure quietly crept up the walkway to Billy's house, and just before reaching the porch, the figure darted to the right to be lost in the shadows of the adjacent house. While out in the street, the figure's car engine ticked softly; the metal cooling in the cool night air.

No one else was about, but if they were, they might have noticed the crickets grow quiet as if they were holding their breath, knowing something bad was coming and unable to stop it.

Chapter Twenty-six

*I*T DIDN'T TAKE Rupert much time to return to Portal Control.

After entering and walking through the vast structure, he sighed upon reaching the actual portal.

Once again a massive line of creatures waited as each one was searched by security.

Checking the clock on the wall, he realized he should have left sooner, but then resigned himself to an hour of waiting in line.

About a dozen feet in front of him, an old creature similar to a giant cat was being stripped searched. The old creature needed a walker to move and was now wearing nothing but its fur.

Rupert rubbed his face with his big paws. Of all the people to be searched, the security guards had picked this old fossil. When they had finally finished—finding nothing unusual—the creature was allowed through.

The line shortened slowly and Rupert passed the time by reading the signs posted around the gate. Multiple signs listed items that were now not allowed through the portal. Items such as nail clippers, toothpaste, and mouthwash were now all banned.

Rupert watched as a small monster that looked a lot like an Earth raccoon took off his shoes and showed the guard there was nothing in them but the creature's feet.

Time passed and it was finally Rupert's turn.

"Do you have anything to declare?" The bored security guard asked.

"Yes I do, what in the world are you idiots doing around here?"

"I'm sorry, sir, but we're just being cautious. Wouldn't want any terrorists to take over the portal."

Rupert made a disgusted noise. "With what? A pair of nail clippers? That's the most ridiculous thing I've heard all day."

The security guard's eyes became slits as he studied Rupert a bit more closely.

"That sounds like terrorist talk to me."

Rupert suddenly realized maybe he had opened his mouth a little too much and tried to flash his most sincere smile at the guard.

"Me? A terrorist? Look, I was just joking, Officer, do you think I could get going?"

The guard looked over at his partner, who shrugged, not caring one way or the other. Luckily, another patron in line yelled at the guard, telling him to hurry up, distracting him from Rupert.

The guard grinned malevolently and called the patron who had yelled at him to step forward and to move to the side of the line.

Now that the guard had a new creature to vent his wrath on, he waved Rupert forward onto the portal platform. Before the portal opened and took him where he needed to go, Rupert was able to catch a brief glance over his shoulder at what was going on.

The creature who had yelled at the guard to speed it up was now being moved behind a curtain and the guard was pulling on a white latex glove.

Then the portal took him and he tried to relax and go with it as his body was sent across dimensions, back to Earth and Timmy.

*　　*　　*

The dark figure huddling near the side of Billy's house looked up and down the side of the small home, trying to discern the best way inside.

Settling on a basement window, he casually kicked the glass in with his foot.

The breaking glass sounded loud in the silence of the night and the figure cringed, cursing himself for being careless.

The figure leaned forward, his ear trying to catch the sound that a neighbor had heard the breaking window, but all remained quiet.

No lights flicked on in the neighboring home's windows, telling him he was safe.

Leaning over to inspect the shattered window, the figure's face fell into a dim ray of moonlight and the grim countenance of David could be seen if anyone was awake and watching him. But alas, the neighboring house remained quiet, and after a moment to see if any lights appeared in Billy's house, he was satisfied he had gotten away with breaking the window.

A stray, fist-sized rock lay near the foundation of the house and David picked it up and used it to clear away any shards of glass from the frame of the window. Once finished, he tossed it to his side and then dropped to his belly.

Feet first, he slid through the window, dropping down to the basement floor. With the wan light seeping in through the small window, he was able to make out a neat and tidy cellar.

Off to his left were a couple of boxes labeled, XMAS, and if there was any doubt to the contents, then the silver strand of garland and the plastic Santa Claus statue peeking from the top box answered his silent question.

To his right was a small workbench, complete with miscellaneous tools all spread out on a plywood wall filled with protruding metal spikes to hang them on. A toaster lay on the bench in multiple pieces, as if the repairman had abandoned it in the middle of fixing it.

In the dim light, David's eyes caught the glint of something silver on the workbench, next to the toaster, and he moved closer to investigate.

Lying innocently on the workbench's flat top was an eight-inch long Bowie knife. Next to the knife were miscellaneous fishing supplies. Evidently, Billy liked to fish, and probably used the survival knife to gut and clean his catch.

Picking the knife up, he slid the blade from its leather sheath, studying the way the polished metal reflected the dim gloom of the cellar. The honed blade seemed to reflect whatever ambient light it could find, almost as if it was drawing the light to it.

With a gleam in his eye and a smirk on his face, David dropped the leather sheath for the blade to the workbench, not needing it, and decided the Bowie knife would be perfect for what he had planned.

All the better if the boy was killed with his grandfather's own knife. Just one more nail in Billy's coffin when the police arrived and found the boy's body.

Creeping across the basement floor, he stopped at a set of wooden stairs. At the top was another door, a soft light spilling under the half-inch crack that separated the door from the floor.

Holding his breath, he stepped onto the first step. Other than a soft creak, the step was silent. One step at a time, hesitating after his weight had compressed the old wood, he slowly skulked up the cellar stairs.

Three minutes later, but what felt like an eternity, David reached out for the door that would allow him access to the first floor of the house.

With his hand on the doorknob, he turned it softly only to find it locked.

Cursing under his breath, he stood there waiting, wondering what he should do now. Though he needed to get rid of Timmy, this breaking and entering, and later, murder, was all new to him.

With his eyes adjusted to the dark, he was able to see a thin line of light seeping through where the door lock met the door frame. Thinking about some movies he'd seen in the past, he decided to see if any of that stuff on the big screen actually worked in real life. Placing the knife's tip where the lock would be, he gently pushed it into the gap.

The blade slid in easily, compressing the lock as simply if he'd used a credit card. The door popped open, and with a slight squeak of hinges, he stepped out onto the first floor.

The house was dark and silent.

No one stirred in their beds. He was just another shadow in a house full of shadows. Looking around himself, he saw he was in the kitchen. The sink was full of dirty dishes and the refrigerator hummed softly.

There was only one way to go further into the house and he followed the small hallway until he came out into the living room.

Holding his breath, he waited, trying to be as careful as possible. It would be almost laughable to make it this far only to come around a corner and walk into Billy as the man got out of bed to use the bathroom or grab a drink of water.

Though dim, there was enough light in the living room for David to easily see the other hallway that led to the bedrooms and bathroom.

Gripping the handle of the blade tighter, he slowly moved toward the first bedroom door. The door was already ajar, and with the toe of his foot, he gently pushed it open a fraction of an inch more.

Though the room was shrouded in darkness, the small shape under the blankets in the room's sole bed was easy to make out.

Nodding to himself that he'd found his target, he backed away from the door and checked the other two doors. One was the bathroom and was ignored, but the other one was Billy's room. The older man was sound asleep, his snoring drifting out into the hallway.

David looked around for something to use as a club, his eyes falling on a small statue of a frog.

Unbeknownst to him, Timmy's grandmother had a thing for frogs, the bedroom and living room covered with the small statues in all shapes and sizes. The one he picked up off a small side table was about six inches tall and four inches wide and made out of a heavy plastic resin.

He weighed it a few times in his hand, deciding the weight was sufficient for the task at hand. Then he opened Billy's door wide and crept into the room.

It was eerie being so close to another person, with said person being oblivious. With his own heart beating in his chest, he sucked in his last breath, and in three strides had crossed the room and was standing over Billy's prone, sleeping body.

Before he could change his mind about what he was about to do and run screaming from the house, he raised the heavy statue over Billy's head and brought it down hard against the man's temple.

Billy shook once in his sleep, his head bouncing on the pillow as it absorbed the blow, and then he remained still.

David stood over him, panting.

His pulse was racing and he realized whatever happened next he would have to see it through to the end. Still, he felt great, alive. This was what man did, despite the fact that man tried to be civilized. When in fact man was nothing more than another animal that needed to hunt and kill.

Before he turned away from Billy's supine body, he noticed the man's chest rising and falling, the movement slow and steady.

David grunted at that.

He struggled with whether he should finish Billy off or not, but finally decided to let the old man live, though not out of any form of mercy.

Fine, he thought. If the man was still alive then all the better for him to take the fall of the boy's murder. But if he was dead that would mean he couldn't contradict what would be happening next.

Damn, he couldn't decide what to do.

David stood over the unconscious body, still wrestling with the idea if he should just kill the man or let him live. His decision was taken from him when he heard Timmy cry out from across the hall.

Turning quickly, David stood perfectly still, sweat pooling in the small of his back and sending a chill up his spine. He waited anxiously, and when the sound wasn't repeated, he believed Timmy was having a nightmare like he would back home.

Ever since the death of his real father, Timmy would sometimes be plagued by nightmares and visions of his father still alive. In the dreams, Timmy's father would talk to him and tell him things.

David let out the breath he was holding, a small portion of relief flooding through him. If he had his way, he would kill the boy quick, slicing his throat from ear to ear. He wasn't exactly relishing the deed now that it was upon him, but his blood was fired up after pummeling Billy. When he had thought about the task days earlier, it had seemed so simple, an easy solution to the problem of the boy talking about his misdeeds. But now he realized taking another life, especially one so small, was much harder than he would have thought.

But he would manage, because the alternative was going to jail for things even he didn't want to admit to.

He shook off his self-doubt.

No, he had to do it. If he didn't, then the little bastard would squeal and David would wind up in prison for molesting him.

And he knew what they did to men like him in prison.

With his mind made up, and his face set with grim determination again, he left Billy's room and headed for Timmy's.

He just had to stay focused and it would all be over in a few minutes.

CHAPTER TWENTY-SEVEN

*T*IMMY WAS DREAMING as he lay in the bed that was once his father's.

Just before he drifted off to sleep, he could almost sense his father's presence in the room. But that would be ridiculous. Ghosts weren't real, they were just something adults thought up to accept the fact that there was something more than simple death after you died. At least that was what Jimmy Monahan said in school.

Jimmy's parents were atheists, and when Timmy had asked his mom to explain it to him one day when she was feeling better--one of her good days--she had tried to teach him what an atheist was.

Timmy had just nodded, only understanding a portion of what she said, but then his mind had drifted off as he thought about the upcoming Spiderman movie coming out in a few months.

But now, as Timmy lay in the bed, the darkness surrounding him, he felt a small amount of comfort thinking that somewhere up in the sky, way past the clouds, his father was watching over him.

So as he slept and dreamed, it was no wonder his father would appear to him.

Robert Conrad stood in a wide open, flat plain filled with tall, waving grass. Timmy was at the other end, and when he realized the man he could barely make out was his father, he started to run toward him, calling out his name.

His father said nothing, but just smiled while he waited for his only son to reach him. But the plain was fraught with peril and as Timmy tried to reach his father, he found deep crevices filled with writhing snakes in his path.

A large, fallen tree was his only way across the dangerous area, and he precariously slid across the tree, his feet always close to slipping on the loose bark and sending him plummeting to his death.

Somehow he knew the snakes were poisonous, and if he was to fall, his body would swell to twice its normal size as the snakes' venom flooded his circulatory system and killed him in utter agony.

But he missed his father and was determined to reach him.

With his heart in his throat, he managed to make it to the other side only to be stopped by two more adults.

He recognized them immediately as Susan and Charlie, the bad grown-ups who had killed children and made them do despicable things to one another.

His father waited beyond them, his standing figure seen easily through the shoulders of the two adults.

Timmy looked down at his feet and saw the ground was littered with rocks.

Summoning even more courage, he retrieved the largest he could pick up and threw them as hard as he could at both Susan and Charlie.

Both adults hissed and snarled, trying to fend off the assault, but in no time both were down on the ground.

Timmy found it odd that there was no blood, and as he stepped over them and moved a few feet passed them, he turned to see their bodies were gone, nothing but a few stray marks to prove he had seen anything at all.

Turning to look at his father, Robert waved and gestured for Timmy to hurry. Timmy didn't know why, but he could almost feel his father's will silently urging him onward.

Timmy started to run again, only to be stopped by the two drug dealers who had wanted to use him for their own gains. Clarence smiled slyly, his teeth flashing in the bright light of the plain.

Slim bent over and prepared himself for Timmy when the boy tried to get by him. Timmy set his jaw and ran as fast as he could at both of them. At the last moment, he danced to the left, causing Slim to fall off balance and tumble to the ground. Timmy never saw any of this, but continued running.

Sparing a brief glance over his shoulder, he saw Clarence watching him, making no attempt to follow. As the black man disappeared from view, Timmy could have sworn the man smiled encouragingly to him, although that could have been a trick of the light.

Timmy continued running, prepared to overcome whatever else was going to come between him and his father, but nothing else would slow him down.

He ran as fast as he could and Robert bent over, ready for his son to leap into his arms.

Timmy did just that, and with a final leap that had him covering four feet of ground, he came to rest inside his father's arms.

Father and son hugged each other and Timmy knew he hadn't felt this happy for a very long time. When Timmy pulled away, still in his father's arms, he saw Robert's face was sad.

"What's wrong, Daddy, why are you sad? Aren't you happy to be with me?" Timmy asked.

Robert nodded slightly. "Of course, Timmy. I can't tell you how much I've missed you, but I can't stay. I've come to you because I have something very important to tell you, so I need you to listen, okay?"

Timmy nodded, not understanding, but just happy to be with his father again.

Robert whispered in his ear and Timmy's face grew cold. When he was finished, he set his son down and knelt beside him.

"I have to go now, son, but remember, I'm always watching you and looking out for you."

Timmy started to cry, not wanting his father to leave.

"No," he cried. "I don't want you to go. I want to come with you."

Robert smiled slightly at that and chuckled. "I'm sorry, kiddo, but you can't come with me, not for a very long time. But someday, I promise, we'll be together again."

Timmy's tears were falling uncontrollably and his vision became blurred.

"You promise?" He sniffed, rubbing his eyes clear, but only smudging his tears further across his cheeks.

Robert cupped his son's face in his hands and nodded. "I promise, now you have to do what I said, okay? The second you wake up, promise me."

Timmy wiped his nose clean of phlegm with his sleeve and nodded to his father.

"I promise, Dad."

Then Robert seemed to float away as if on a light breeze. Timmy held up his hands as if he could reach out and pull his father to his breast with his will alone, but soon realized it was hopeless. This was one of those things his mother had told him he couldn't control, no matter how hard he wanted to.

"Don't forget, I love you and will always be with you," Robert said, his ghostly form vanishing into the air.

Timmy fell to his knees and cried then, his head falling onto his lap. He had been so happy one moment and an instant later all had changed. Now he missed his father more than ever, the pain of his loss sharp, like a knife wound that was almost healed only to be ripped open once more.

Alone in the field of grass, he sobbed until he felt he had nothing left to cry.

When his tears had dried he stood and looked around himself.

He was alone again, not even the terrors he had overcome to get to his father were there to keep him company. With his head held low, he walked away, not knowing where he was going, but just wanting to move.

When he reached the edge of the plain there was nothing but blackness, like God had created the world and had stopped at a certain point where there was nothing but a void.

Curiosity getting the better of him, he stepped off the plain, his foot seeming to be standing on nothing. It was as if there was a glass platform only he could traverse.

Deciding he had nothing to lose, he continued out into the void, not knowing where he was going, but as he became farther away from the edge of the plain, he started to worry. His grief over his father was lost as his own will for survival took front row in his mind.

Deciding he had made a bad call, he turned around to start back when his foot came down on nothing. His body fell forward and he found himself plummeting downward into darkness. He called out for his father to save him, but knew it was too late.

With a scream in his throat, he plummeted into oblivion.

Timmy snapped awake, the feeling of falling still in the pit of his stomach. He blinked his eyes in the darkness, straining to see anything.

At first all was quiet, but as his mind became more focused, pushing the dreams to the back of his mind, he realized there was something wrong in the house.

Footsteps could be heard coming from the hallway and then distinct sound of heavy breathing came to his ears.

His father's voice came to him from the shadows in the room, telling him to get up and move, then the voice was gone like a wisp of smoke in a strong wind.

Slipping out of the bed, Timmy padded over to the bedroom door.

With his ear close to the opening, he strained to hear what had apparently woken him up.

Wondering if it was just his grandpa, he was about to call out, when his nose started to twitch. He smelled the distinct aroma of aftershave.

And not just any aftershave; it was OLD SPICE.

Deep in his subconscious, something more from his dream floated to forefront of his mind. He remembered his dad then, and in his dream he had told Timmy something.

Something important.

His father had told him to wake up and run. Run away as fast as he could!

The breathing on the other side of the door grew louder and the door started to open, the oiled hinges making no sound.

Timmy was petrified; somehow his worst fear had found him. He had traveled across multiple states to escape him, overcome many perils, but as difficult as it was to admit, his step-father was on the other side of his bedroom door!

Timmy's heart beat so fast he thought it would explode out of his chest, and as the door opened inward, he slowly retreated away from it.

When the door was half-open, the intruder prepared to enter and Timmy received a flash from his dream.

Galvanized to action, he backed away from the door and then charged into it, putting his entire small frame behind the rush.

The wooden door slammed shut, striking the shadow-enshrouded figure hard. Something dropped from the intruder's hand and a curse issued from his mouth. That was when Timmy knew it was David, the unmistakable voice burned into his memory forever.

David fell away from the door, not expecting it to snap back into him. His wrist hurt as the knife was knocked to the floor, the balanced blade sticking into the wood only a hair's-breath from the tip of his left shoe.

Then a small blur darted past him as Timmy ran through the unblocked doorway and out into the hallway.

David cursed again, then bent over to retrieve his lost blade, and with weapon in hand, went on the hunt for Timmy.

Chapter Twenty-eight

*T*IMMY DASHED DOWN the short hallway into his grandfather's room. Tears of terror were already falling from his eyes as he ran up to Billy's bed and pulled on the unconscious man's arm.

"Grandpa, you have to get up! David's in the house and he wants to hurt me!" He screamed. Then he stopped tugging on his arm, and in the dim light of the room, he saw the dark wet spot on Billy's pillow.

"Grandpa, are you okay?" He asked, his hand reaching out to touch the blood which had dripped from the messy head wound on his temple.

Timmy's breathing stopped when he thought he was looking at his dead grandfather. He backed away from him in shock, not having any idea what he should do, where he should go now.

Then he heard the distinct sound of heavy footsteps coming from his bedroom. He looked around frantically, trying to think of where to hide; anywhere was good at the moment. Finally, he decided to go under his grandfather's bed.

Dropping to all fours, he quickly slid under the bed, the sheets and blankets covering him as his feet disappeared.

His nose wrinkled from all the dust-bunnies under the bed; evidently his grandma wasn't much of a housekeeper. His nose twitched and he thought he was going to sneeze from all the dust when he saw a set of legs step into the room.

David took only one step inside the dark room, this time wary of the open door.

"Come out, you little bastard. I just want to talk to you about a few things," he growled as he hovered by the door. "I promise I won't hurt you…much."

Once he knew the door was clear, he stepped inside the room, blocking the only way out.

Timmy stayed perfectly still, his pulse beating in his temple like a set of bongo drums. He didn't have to sneeze anymore, knowing if he gave away his location, he was doomed. He had no way of knowing David wanted to kill him, but the thoughts that went through an eight-year-old's brain were almost as bad.

To Timmy, death was better than being caught by David.

David crept into the room, and immediately noticed the half-open closet. The man darted across the room, ripping the closet open and stabbing into the hanging clothes with his Bowie knife, but all he managed to kill was an imitation fur coat.

With David on the other side of the room, Timmy decided he needed to move now while the doorway was clear. Crawling out from under the bed, he stayed on all fours until he was at the doorway. He had to open the door, which had partially closed when David had pushed it in, and when the door creaked on its hinges, David's head swiveled like an owl's to see his prey ready to escape.

"There you are!" He snarled "Get back here, you little shit," he spit while moving across the room to reach the door. But Timmy was already gone, having slipped back into the hallway, his bare feet slapping hard on the polished wood as he ran.

He bolted straight to the front door, planning on opening it and running outside for help, but the deadbolt was tricky. Billy had dealt with it for years and knew just how to lift up and twist at the same time. But Timmy was smaller and had no way of knowing this. The door stayed locked, and no matter how hard Timmy tried to unlock it, the worn lock held fast.

Heavy footsteps sounded behind him and he turned to see David charge into the room. Timmy's eyes went wide when he saw the Bowie knife gleam in the wan light. His mind pieced together everything that had happened and he realized he wasn't going to just receive a beating if David caught him.

Oh no, he thought. David planned to do him real harm!

Timmy ran for the couch, putting the worn piece of furniture between him and David. Every time David would try to circle around it, Timmy would just move the opposite way.

Stalemate.

"What are you doing here, Timmy? Why did you come all the way to Boston?" David asked, breathing heavily.

Timmy was terrified, but something from his dream, something his father had said gave him strength.

"You know why, David. To get away from you. What did you do to my grandpa?"

David shrugged casually. "Not much; just introduced his head to a frog. You know, I never liked the old bastard that much. Always sticking his nose where it didn't belong. When I married your mom, both you and her became my family. I sure as hell didn't need a dead guy's parents always butting into my business."

Timmy's eyes flared with anger. "They're my grandparents and they're my family, not like you, you're a perve!" He yelled.

One of his friends at school had used the word and Timmy had found out what it meant. It seemed appropriate now.

David's face went ashen. "Why, you little shit, when I get my hands on you!" He lunged over the couch, trying to catch Timmy before he could run, but the boy was faster.

Not knowing where to run, he ran back the way he'd come, back towards his room. As he ran inside the small room and slammed the door closed behind him, he realized he just made a terrible mistake.

He was trapped!

He was so frightened of David catching up to him, he never thought of the window behind him, an easy way to escape the room.

He leaned against the door, making sure to press the small button on the doorknob to lock the door, and breathing heavily, knowing it would only be a matter of seconds before the door bucked from David trying to force his way into the room.

He prayed for someone to help him.

Realizing his small frame could never stop David from knocking down the door, but not knowing what else to do, he stayed perfectly still, some shred of hope imagining David just giving up and leaving the house.

That was when his eyes spied the window, but before he could even think of using it, the door shook on its frame.

"Little pigs, little pigs, let me in or I'll friggin' kill ya!" David yelled, playing with his prey. He struck the door again and Timmy's teeth rattled from the blow.

The next impact would force the door in and David would have him.

His heart sank and he started to cry again. He felt so lost and without hope, especially after all he'd been through, only to have it end like this.

It wasn't fair!

The door shook again, and managed to hold, but Timmy knew his luck had run out. Stepping away from the door, he walked over to his bed, sat down and faced the door. He looked down at his pile of clothes spread out on the floor and suddenly realized he was still in his underwear.

A moment later the door was smashed in, falling off one of its hinges and cracking down the middle.

His chest heaving, David stood triumphant, "I've got you, you little shit, there's nowhere to run and no one to help you!"

Timmy sighed and let the tears come unbidden as David crossed the few feet separating him from Timmy, preparing to end the chase once and for all.

Chapter Twenty-nine

*T*IMMY WATCHED HELPLESSLY as his step-father crossed the small distance from the door to his bed.

David grinned malevolently and raised the Bowie knife high over his head, prepared to bring it down in an overhand strike that would slice Timmy in twain.

Timmy stared at the blade, unable to look away even though he knew it was the instrument of his death.

But just as David was about to bring his arm down, a white light appeared from under the bed and David was pulled off his feet.

Two large purple paws with claws wrapped themselves around his shins and yanked as hard as they could.

David was thrown backward, the knife flying from his hand. As he fell, his head struck the hanging door, the doorknob striking his head enough to give him a light concussion.

Lying flat on his back on the floor, looking up at the dark ceiling, he tried to clear his fuzzy vision. His mind was working slowly, as if in a fog, and for the life of himself, he had no possible idea how he had managed to end up on the floor.

He felt a tugging at his feet and he bent his head up, looking downward…and screamed.

What looked like a giant, purple bear was pulling him under the bed!

While one eye on the creature drooped slightly, the teeth in its mouth were apparently long and sharp.

David started to scream and shriek as his fingers reached out to somehow halt his backward descent. Hands wrapped around a throw rug, but it was tossed aside as useless. His nails scratched the hardwood floor as he was inexorably pulled under the bed.

Screaming until he was hoarse, his eyes went wide when he saw some kind of spinning hole under the bed. The purple monster was on the edge of the void, balancing precariously, and with one final yank, David was pulled under the bed where he then dropped into the swirling black hole.

He let out one more ear-piercing scream and then he was gone.

The portal closed with a pop and Rupert climbed out from under the bed.

Timmy's eyes went wide with surprise.

"Rupert, you came back and saved me!" He said, running into the creature's arms.

Rupert wrapped Timmy in a protective hug and picked him up.

"Of course I did, silly. I told you I'd be back. I didn't follow you all over the place to let you get hurt now, did I. What kind of friend would I be if I did?"

Timmy hugged him again and buried his face in the soft fur. "That was my step-dad and he wanted to hurt me. If you hadn't gotten here when you did…" Timmy trailed off and Rupert rubbed his back.

"Its okay, Timmy, you're safe now. David won't be bothering you again, I promise."

Timmy pulled away from Rupert, and blinked at him, now curious.

"Rupert, where did David go?"

Rupert sighed. "Well, Timmy, I sent him to my world."

"Really? But I thought humans couldn't go there. Can I go there, too?" Timmy asked, hoping beyond hope.

Rupert set Timmy on the bed and knelt down next to him. "No, pal, I'm afraid you can't. I'm gonna end up owing a few monsters a couple of favors for sending David to Monster City. In fact, if I didn't get a raise, I probably wouldn't have been able to do it at all."

Timmy nodded, sort of understanding. "But how did you grab him, I thought you couldn't touch anyone but me?"

Rupert nodded as he stood back up. "That's true, Timmy, but if I focus all my energy into one moment, I can touch another human for a brief instant, like I did when I grabbed David's legs. Believe me, it takes a lot out of me, I'm exhausted."

Timmy decided he didn't care how it had happened, just that it did, and he hugged Rupert again.

Then a groan sounded from out in the hall and Timmy looked up.

"Oh my God, that's my grandpa. He's alive!" He said, running out of the bedroom and into Billy's room.

"Grandpa, are you alive?" Timmy asked.

Billy rubbed his head and groaned again. He tried to blink his vision clear, but at the moment he was seeing double. Rupert followed Timmy and stood in the doorway.

Billy turned to look at his grandson and winced as he touched the large lump on his temple. "What happened? What the hell hit me?" He moaned.

"It was David, he snuck in here and hit you with a frog and then he tried to kill me, but my friend Rup…"

Rupert stopped him at that. "Hold up there, Timmy, don't say anything about me. No one will believe you, just say that David got scared and ran away."

Timmy turned to Rupert, nodded slightly, and then turned back to Billy.

Billy never noticed the break in the conversation, still dazed from his head wound.

"I knew those damn frogs your grandmother collected would be the death of me. But wait, where's David now?" He asked and then let Timmy continue.

"I guess he got scared and decided to leave," he said almost idly and then he jumped onto Billy's lap and hugged him. "Oh, Grandpa, I thought you were dead!"

Billy tried to laugh at that, but it just made his head hurt. Finally, he tried to sit a little more and when a wave of dizziness had passed, he did just that.

"It'll take a lot more than a bump on the noggin' to get rid of me. Now help me up, I think we should call the police."

Timmy did as he was told and together they made it to the kitchen phone. After a quick call to the police to report the break-in, and a quick bag of ice for Billy's head wound, which looked worse than it was, as head wounds usually do, Billy sat down at the kitchen table and rested while Timmy excused himself for a minute.

Rupert had told Timmy he needed to leave and gestured for Timmy to follow him out of the kitchen. Rupert and Timmy walked back to the bedroom and in hushed tones, so his grandpa wouldn't hear, Timmy said goodbye to Rupert.

"Do you really have to go?"

"I'm afraid so, Timmy. My job is to scare kids and I think you're way past that, don't you think?"

"Yeah, I guess so. Will I ever see you again?"

Rupert shrugged. "Who knows what the future will bring, but for now, I think you'll be fine on your own. You have a great grandfather there and you know your mom loves you."

Timmy frowned, sad to see his friend leave. "Yeah, I guess so, but it was so cool having my very own monster."

Rupert pressed a button in his pocket and the portal flashed open under the bed a second later.

Rupert crawled under the bed and turned and waved goodbye. "Bye, Timmy, now promise me, no more running away."

Timmy smiled back and waved. "Okay, Rupert, I promise. Besides, I wasn't running away from anything. I was running to my grandpa, and now that I'm here, I'm not going anywhere."

Rupert grinned. "That's very good, Timmy, you're wise beyond your years. Well, goodbye, I'll miss you, be good." Then he dropped through the portal and was gone.

Timmy stood perfectly still, watching as the light from the portal disappeared. Then he was alone again in his room.

But this time he wasn't really alone. He had his grandparents and a mother who would be arriving soon to take care of him. Without David pushing pills on her, she would realize what had happened to her and become better, her and Timmy living happily ever after together.

Though Timmy didn't know it yet, his future looked bright. But for now he was just an eight-year-old boy with a monster under the bed for a friend.

With a wide smile across his face, and a feeling of contentment in his heart, Timmy left the bedroom to join his grandfather in the kitchen.

Epilogue

*D*AVID BLACKED OUT as his body was ripped apart and sent across time and space. Feeling light-headed, he slowly regained consciousness and upon opening his eyes, he gasped at what was looking down on him.

He was in some kind of building, and a white light swirled in front of him, but it was the two creatures that were hovering over him that made him scream in terror.

Jumping to his feet, he backed away from the two portal security guards only to bump into some other form of monster.

"Hey, watch-it, pal, I'm walkin' here," a crab-like creature said in a Brooklyn accent.

David said nothing, still in shock to what he was seeing. While he backed away from the crab creature, he mentally tried to piece together what was happening to him.

Had Timmy somehow slipped him a drug, such as LSD, and he was even now lying on the floor of the house with Timmy while his mind went on some kind of psychedelic adventure?

Then a voice from behind him called out and pointed at him. It was the purple creature that had pulled him into the void at Timmy's house.

"Hey, you guys, stop him, you can't just let him run around like that?" Rupert yelled as he materialized on the portal platform.

David's shock broke and he ran for the opening at the end of the lobby.

Creatures flew by him and some called out to him, unused to seeing a human on their world, but David ignored them.

How could they be real?

How could any of this be real?

Somehow assuming once he left the building things would be better, he charged through the large glass doors and out into the street.

As he looked around at the odd looking monsters that walked by on the relatively mundane sidewalk, and the cars that were similar to earth's automobiles, he realized that running outside might not have been one of the best choices to make.

Rupert stepped off the platform and looked at guard number one.

"Why didn't you grab him? We can't have a human running around out there!" Rupert chastised the creature.

The guard shrugged. "You're yelling at me? What made you decide to bring a human here? That's a big no-no."

Rupert thought about Cecil, the head monster and his deal with him.

"Let's just say I've got connections high up, besides, what's one human going to do?"

Guard number two chuckled. "Nothing, except become dinner for another monster, that's what."

Rupert's eyes went wide. "Oh, no, I didn't think of that. I've got to catch him." Then he took off at a distance-eating run, his muscular legs carrying him across the open lobby. Reaching the outside doors in moments, and disappearing out onto the street, he was nothing but a purple blur.

Guard one looked at guard two. "You think he'll find him?"

Guard two gave him a look of indifference. "Don't know, don't care, I'm going on my break."

As the guard left, the other guard got back to work. A line had begun to form and he needed to keep things moving.

David ran down a side street, the sounds and faces of the creatures around him making him scream constantly.

How could this be real? It was all so impossible.

It was all a nightmare and he would wake up in a minute and realize he was still safe in his bed and he had never left Virginia.

Creatures from his nightmares flowed past him and he ducked into a doorway to take a breather. Despite the few odd looks from the walking, crawling, and sometimes rolling, creatures, moving past him on the sidewalk, none of them seemed to care about him; that was his only saving grace.

Then he heard a yell from behind him and looked to see the purple monster running after him; the one from Timmy's room.

That creature seemed to want him bad and David wasn't about to wait around to find out why.

His imagination did that for him as gory images of the creature using those big purple claws to tear him apart limb from limb to feast on his insides.

No way was that going to happen to him, so he ran, and ran and ran.

*   *   *

Slowing down with his chest heaving from exhaustion, David leaned against a building. He had no way of knowing how far he'd run or where he was.

Luckily, it appeared he had lost the purple creature, somehow losing him in the crowded and winding streets.

He needed to find a place to hide, to gather his wits and figure out what to do next, when he saw a large creature walking toward him.

It was covered in white fur and had on what appeared to be lipstick. As the creature crossed the street and moved closer to him, he thought the monster resembled a large grizzly bear.

It was odd seeing this creature walking around on two legs and digging into a large purse at her side like any woman from Earth would do.

He stood perfectly still.

If the creature was like the others he'd seen, then hopefully it would merely look at him with curiosity and move on.

Mrs. Mellanger saw the strange looking, pink-skinned creature and immediately knew what it was. She was a secretary for one of the major firms in Monster City, and though she had never actually seen a human up close before, she knew what they looked like.

She marveled at the lack of fur and the skinny limbs.

When she was only a few feet from the small man, she stopped and looked down at him.

"Why, hello there dear, are you all right. You know, you really shouldn't be walking around the streets alone; it's dangerous."

David blinked up at the creature.

The voice, though deep, reminded him of his grandmother, the voice soft and caring. Her soothing voice placed him at ease and it was the first time since he had arrived in this strange place that he actually wasn't totally petrified.

"You're talking to me? Nicely? Uhm, I don't know what to say. You're the first creature to say anything remotely pleasant to me or act like I matter."

Mrs. Mellanger patted his shoulder gently. "That's okay, dear, it's just that most of us have never seen a human before, it's quite a shock. If you'd like to come inside with me, I'll be happy to help you." She pointed to the building he was leaning against. "I live in here. I have a beautiful apartment. Would you like to see it?"

David didn't answer, but stood perfectly still. Other creatures moved around them, some so hideous he had only imagined them in his worst nightmares.

A seven foot, five-legged squid-like creature sloshed by and slowed as it passed him. Its orifice opened wide and three rows of teeth glistened in the sun, making David want to pee himself in fright.

That made up his mind for him and he nodded to the white bear creature.

"Wonderful," she said and led him into the lobby and to the elevators.

David stared at Ralph as they moved through the lobby, the slug doorman reading a newspaper behind his desk. Ralph glanced up, nodded politely as the two of them walked by him, and then returned to his reading, as if a human in his lobby was no big deal.

Stepping into the elevator, Mrs. Mellanger smiled as the doors began to close.

"You'll love my place, dear, but I hope you don't mind if I have a bite to eat when we get there, I'm starving."

David shook his head slowly, lost in his own befuddlement of everything happening to him. "No, I don't mind, go nuts."

As the elevator doors slid closed on greased hinges, David saw his reflection in the shiny panels, and the reflection of Mrs. Mellanger. She noticed him watching her and she smiled sweetly, the look giving David the chills.

As the elevator shot downward, deep underground, David had the feeling he was taking an elevator ride to Hell.

He was so distracted by the flashing numbers as the car surged ever downward, he never saw the feral grin on Mrs. Mellanger's face as her tongue slipped out and she licked her ruby red lips.

She had never had human before and was very much looking forward to having some exotic cuisine for a change.

DEAD RECKONING: DAWNING OF THE DEAD
By Anthony Giangregorio

THE DEAD HAVE RISEN!

In the dead city of Pittsburgh, two small enclaves struggle to survive, eking out an existence of hand to mouth.

But instead of working together, both groups battle for the last remaining fuel and supplies of a city filled with the living dead.

Six months after the initial outbreak, a lone helicopter arrives bearing two more survivors and a newborn baby. One enclave welcomes them, while the other schemes to steal their helicopter and escape the decaying city.

With no police, fire, or social services existing, the two will battle for dominance in the steel city of the walking dead.

But when the dust settles, the question is: will the remaining humans be the winners, or the losers?

When the dead walk, the line between Heaven and Hell is so twisted and bent there is no line at all.

RISE OF THE DEAD
By Anthony Giangregorio

DEATH IS ONLY THE BEGINNING

In less than forty-eight hours, more than half the globe was infected.

In another forty-eight, the rest would be enveloped.

The reason?

A science experiment gone horribly wrong which enabled the dead to walk, their flesh rotting on their bones even as they seek human prey.

Jeremy was an ordinary nineteen year old slacker. He partied too much and had done poorly in high school. After a night of drinking and drugs, he awoke to find the world a very different place from the one he'd left the night before.

The dead were walking and feeding on the living, and as Jeremy stepped out into a world gone mad, the dead spotting him alone and unarmed in the middle of the street, he had to wonder if he would live long enough to see his twentieth birthday.

BOOK 6

DEAD UNION
By Anthony Giangregorio

BRAVE NEW WORLD

More than a year has passed since the world died not with a bang, but with a moan.
Where sprawling cities once stood, now only the dead inhabit the hollow walls of a shattered civilization; a mockery of lives once led.
But there are still survivors in this barren world, all slowly struggling to take back what was stripped from their birthright; the promise of a world free of the undead.
Fortified towns have shunned the outside world, becoming massive fortresses in their own right. These refugees of a world torn asunder are once again trying to carve out a new piece of the earth, or hold onto what little they already possess.

HOSTAGES

Henry Watson and his warrior survivalists are conscripted by a mad colonel, one of the last military leaders still functioning in the decimated United States. The colonel has settled in Fort Knox, and from there plans to rule the world with his slave army of lost souls and the last remaining soldiers of a defunct army.
But first he must take back America and mold it in his own image; and he will crush all who oppose him, including the new recruits of Henry and crew.
The battle lines are drawn with the fate of America at stake, and this time, the outcome may be unsure.
In a world where the dead walk, even the grave isn't safe.

THE DARK
By Anthony Giangregorio

DARKNESS FALLS

The darkness came without warning.

First New York, then the rest of United States, and then the world became enveloped in a perpetual night without end.

With no sunlight, eventually the planet will wither and die, bringing on a new Ice Age. But that isn't problem for the human race, for humanity will be dead long before that happens.

There is something in the dark, creatures only seen in nightmares, and they are on the prowl.

Evolution has changed and man is no longer the dominant species.

When we are children, we are told not to fear the dark, that what we believe to exist in the shadows is false.

Unfortunately, that is no longer true.

ANOTHER EXCITING CHAPTER IN THE DEADWATER SERIES!

DEADRAIN
By Anthony Giangregorio

Welcome to the New America, population: 0

When a bacterial outbreak contaminates America's lower atmosphere, the resulting rain mutates into a deadly conduit for death.

Human's all over America are exposed and within a matter of days society has crumbled and the walking dead rule the land.

The America we know is gone, replaced by a new order; where the dead walk and humans are the prey.

Henry Watson and his small group of companions travel the country, searching for someplace better, someplace where the rain is safe.

In the New America the rules have changed; survive or perish.

DARK PLACES
By Anthony Giangregorio

A cave-in inside the Boston subway unleashes something that should have stayed buried forever.

Three boys sneak out to a haunted junkyard after dark and find more than they gambled on.

In a world where everyone over twelve has died from a mysterious illness, one young boy tries to carry on.

A mysterious man in black tries his hand at a game of chance at a local carnival, to interesting results.

God, Allah, and Buddha play a friendly game of poker with the fate of the Earth resting in the balance.

Ever have one of those days where everything that can go wrong, does? Well, so did Byron, and no one should have a day like this!

Thad had an imaginary friend named Charlie when he was a child. Charlie would make him do bad things. Now Thad is all grown up and guess who's coming for a visit?

These and other short stories, all filled with frozen moments of dread and wonder, will keep you captivated long into the night.

Just be sure to watch out when you turn off the light!

DEAD TALES: SHORT STORIES TO DIE FOR
By Anthony Giangregorio

In a world much like our own, terrorists unleash a deadly dis-ease that turns people into flesh-eating ghouls.

A camping trip goes horribly wrong when forces of evil seek to dominate mankind.

After losing his life, a man returns reincarnated again and again; his soul inhabiting the bodies of animals.

In the Colorado Mountains, a woman runs for her life, stalked by a sadistic killer.

In a world where the Patriot Act has come to fruition, a man struggles to survive, despite eroding liberties.

Not able to accept his wife's death, a widower will cross into the dream realm to find her again, despite the dark forces that hold her in thrall.

These and other short stories will captivate and thrill you.

These are short stories to die for.

DEADFREEZE
By Anthony Giangregorio

THIS IS WHAT HELL WOULD BE LIKE IF IT FROZE OVER.

When an experimental serum for hypothermia goes horribly wrong, a small research station in the middle of Antarctica becomes overrun with an army of the frozen dead.

Now a small group of survivors must battle the arctic weather and a horde of frozen zombies as they make their way across the frozen plains of Antarctica to a neighboring research station.

What they don't realize is that they are being hunted by an entity whose sole reason for existing is vengeance; and it will find them wherever they run.

DEADFALL
By Anthony Giangregorio

It's Halloween in the small suburban town of Wakefield, Mass.

While parents take their children trick or treating and others throw costume parties, a swarm of meteorites enter the earth's atmosphere and crash to earth.

Inside are small parasitic worms, no larger than maggots.

The worms quickly infect the corpses at a local cemetery and so begins the rise of the undead.

The walking dead soon get the upper hand, with no one believing the truth.

That the dead now walk.

Will a small group of survivors live through the zombie apocalypse?

Or will they, too, succumb to the Deadfall.

SOULEATER
By Anthony Giangregorio

Twenty years ago, Jason Lawson witnessed the brutal death of his father by something only seen in nightmares, something so horrible he'd blocked it from his mind.

Now twenty years later the creature is back, this time for his son.

Jason won't let that happen.

He'll travel to the demon's world, struggling every second to rescue his son from its clutches.

But what he doesn't know is that the portal will only be open for a finite time and if he doesn't return with his son before it closes, then he'll be trapped in the demon's dimension forever.

DEAD RAGE

By Anthony Giangregorio

An unknown virus spreads across the globe, turning ordinary people into bloodthirsty, ravenous killers.

Only a small percentage of the population is immune and soon become prey to the infected.

Amongst the infected comes a man, stricken by the virus, yet still retaining his grasp on reality. His need to destroy the *normals* becomes an obsession and he raises an army of killers to seek out and kill all who aren't *changed* like himself.

A few survivors gather together on the outskirts of Chicago and find themselves running for their lives as the specter of death looms over all.

The Dead Rage virus will find you, no matter where you hide.

Also available as The Rage Plague by Permuted Press.

THE NEXT EXCITING CHAPTER IN THE DEADWATER SERIES!
BOOK 7

DEAD VALLEY

by Anthony Giangregorio

Untouched Majesty

After nearly drowning in the icy waters of the Colorado River, the six weary companions come upon a beautiful valley nestled in the mountains of Colorado, where the undead plague appears to have never happened.

With the mountains protecting the valley, the deadly rain never fell, and the valley is as untouched as the day it was created.

But the group is soon captured by a secret, military research base now run by a few remaining scientists and soldiers.

On this base, unholy experiments are being carried out, and the group soon finds themselves caught in the middle of it.

Mary, Sue, Raven and Cindy are taken away to be used as breeders, the scientists wanting to create a new utopia, which the living dead can't reach, but the side effect of this is the women will lose their lives.

Henry and Jimmy, now separated and captured themselves, must find a way to save them before it's too late; the scientists unleashing every conceivable mutation at their disposal to stop them.

In the world of the living dead, the past is gone and the future is non-existent.

LIVING DEAD PRESS

Where the Dead Walk

www.livingdeadpress.com